THE
LIVING
SEA
OF
WAKING
DREAMS

THE
LIVING
SEA
OF
WAKING
DREAMS

RICHARD FLANAGAN

KNOPF

KNOPF

UK | USA | Canada | Ireland | Australia
India | New Zealand | South Africa | China

Knopf is part of the Penguin Random House group of companies whose
addresses can be found at global.penguinrandomhouse.com

 Penguin
Random House
Australia

First published by Knopf in 2020

Copyright © Richard Flanagan 2020

The moral right of the author has been asserted.

Front jacket photograph courtesy of plainpicture/wpsteinheisser
Case photography courtesy of Shutterstock
Author photograph by Joel Saget
Jacket and case design by Adam Laszczuk © Penguin Random House
Australia Pty Ltd
Internal design by Post Pre-press Group, Australia
Typeset in 12/16.5 pt Bembo by Post Pre-press Group

Printed and bound in Australia by Griffin Press, part of Ovato, an accredited
ISO AS/NZS 14001 Environmental Management Systems printer

 A catalogue record for this
book is available from the
National Library of Australia

ISBN 978 1 76089 994 3
penguin.com.au

For David and Diane Masters
—lighthouse keepers—

To the axe of the spoiler and self-interest fell a prey;
And Crossberry Way and old Round Oak's narrow lane
With its hollow trees like pulpits, I shall never see again:
Inclosure like a Bonaparte let not a thing remain,
It levelled every bush and tree and levelled every hill
And hung the moles for traitors—though the brook is running still,
It runs a naked brook, cold and chill.

— *John Clare*, 'Remembrances'

ONE

ONE

1

Her hand.

2

It's impossible to say how the vanishing began or if it was already ended, thought Anna. Or, for that matter, how to begin. Whether it's about me or her or him, whether it's she or we or you, whether it's now or then or sometime soon. And not having even the right voice tense pronoun makes it so much harder. Perhaps even impossible. Were words? as Francie pointed.

Well: were they *what*?

As if they too were already then falling apart, so much ash and soot soon to fall, so much smoke to suck down. As if all that can be said is we say you or if that then. Them us were we you?

Maybe Francie is happier not being able t-t-to say anything, Tommy stutters. I mean, is translating experience into words an achievement at all? Or is it just the cause of all our unhappiness? Is it our tragedy and our ongoing conceit? The world gets carried away with words, phrases, and elaborate paragraphs. One word leads to another and soon enough you have affairs, wars, genocide and the Anthropocene. Silence, according to Tommy when in his cups, is the only place where truth can be found.

And what do we have instead? Noise—babble everywhere.

4

For a long time he had been aware of a growing scream that was within him and outside him, continued Anna's brother. He tried to contain that scream, it made him stutter, but it kept insisting. The world grew daily hotter and smokier and nightly noisier: more construction noise more insects disappearing, more road noise more fish stocks collapsing, more news noise more frogs and snakes dying out, more brexitrump climatecoal more and more, more and more fucking tourists everywhere, even here in Tasmania even here at the end of the world, well they were queueing at the top of Everest what could you expect?—more jackhammers more reversing trucks and falling and rising cherry pickers *b-b-beeping*, more tourist coaches clogging small streets more rolling suitcases *click-clack-clacking* in the street more Winifuckingbagos more airbnfuckingbs more locals sleeping in tents all around the city until even his dreams filled with a nightmare of noise movement growth that seemed to benefit no one and only grew things that left people unsettled unhappy that made people poorer; an ever greater panic expressed as movement, a fear of stillness, tourism that was meant to save the island had become the very opposite, tourists even shat in the front yards of locals what the fuck was that saying? They're pulling poor fucking penguins out of their holes holding them up for selfies to Instagram, who were these people? They came in budget flights they came in cruise liners—every year larger, louder and more childish death stars betopped with ever bigger water slides bungee jumps and video screens pushing out just beneath their haze of bunker fuel smoke forced *hap-hap-happy*, says Tommy. Far-far-fucking penitentiaries f-f-faking fun floating over Hobart looks like Noddytown does everyone want to be seven?

Yes no maybe.

5

Just over the mountain behind the city the fires are burning ever closer, every day news reports social media feeds pictures of evacuation centres crowded with hundreds of people it was like a war they were like refugees it was a war and they were losing who was winning who? On his phone the government was calling for more coalmines new coal-fired power stations they'd jail you for twenty-one years if you protested the same as murder now in Australia for calling bullshit on fire they couldn't get enough fire and smoke but he was scared, in truth, he was t-t-terrified, he had had enough. Tasmania was where you came to get away from all that shit but now it was even here, ancient forests vanishing, beaches covered in crap, wild birds vomiting supermarket shopping bags, a world disappearing some terrible violence returning for a final reckoning.

How what why who?

6

And as there was more and more of all these things, says Tommy, there seemed less and less of the world maybe less and less of him. The ladybirds *gone* soldier beetles bluebottles *gone* earwigs you never saw now *gone* beautiful brilliantly coloured Christmas beetles whose gaudy metallic shells they collected as kids *gone* flying ant swarms *gone* frog call in spring cicada drone in summer *gone gone* giant emperor gum moths big as tiny birds, powdery Persian rug wings thrumming of a summer night *gone* and all around them the quolls potoroos pardalotes swift parrots *going going going*. There was way less of everything, says Tommy, she should come with him crayfishing why would anyone? The great kelp forests *gone* abalone *gone* crayfish *gone! Gone! Gone!* Something was wrong he felt it as a pain as a sickness growing within him, growing going gone, a tightness of chest and flesh a shallowness of breathing, day after day night after night. You hear it you can't stop hearing you know?

7

Did she think the problem was love? No one knows how to love was love gone? was it? His own heart felt smaller than a phone, did she know what he means did she know did she?

8

Anna told Tommy he did go on. But she felt it. She felt it eating her. She felt something going. But what was it? She felt her phone vibrate. What happened? What went wrong? Sorry, Tommy, Anna said. She just need want escape this that just check sorry something everything anything.

Tommy went to a Marist Fathers' boarding school at Burnie. Burnie: port, paper-pulp mill, pigment plant, p-p-paedophiles. Came home with a stammer after his twelfth birthday. Tommy drank. Ronnie went to Marist too. Maybe Ronnie would have drunk even more. They talked about Ronnie a lot, certain stories, but not the story, never the story, they talked about his ways, his simple little sayings and tics, his beloved toys and Bup his dog, but mostly they talked about Ronnie's future.

Anna Tommy Ronnie Terzo, each more or less two years apart in that order, and Ronnie, they told each other, the most gifted of them all. Great athlete. Great mind. Maybe yes maybe no maybe he lived, Anna said, maybe he became very fat maybe he drank maybe he died of a brain haemorrhage when he was forty-seven. It wouldn't matter when he died though because he was the most gifted of the four children and he would still be dead, one hundred and thirty-two kilos of precisely nothing precisely dead, forty-seven or fourteen did it matter when?

That's how Ronnie's brothers and sister talked about him, in a circle that went nowhere, but spiralled only inwards, inventing alternative futures for their brother. They called it ronnying. A vortex. A vortex of ronnying.

Tommy said that he couldn't save him. Tommy always said that as though he could have saved him, but Tommy couldn't even save himself. It was for the best,

Tommy would say. And he would start ronnying again. Ronnying and ronnying. It was for the best it was for the worst whatever.

Whatfuckenever.

10

He would like to be reborn, Tommy confessed, as a tree, which tells you as much as you really need to know about Tommy. Anna said if he were a tree today he would be burning and Tommy says he already is. His son, Anna's nephew Davy, is a schizophrenic and is tormented by voices, which is to say words, says Tommy. Tommy worries—obviously—and maintains the battle to love is the battle to keep words at bay, a battle his son lost.

11

Perhaps that is why when Francie asked her what had happened to her hand, Anna said nothing. She put in front of their mother the cup of slurry they agreed to use the word *tea* to describe, thickened to a gel so that she wouldn't drown drinking it, and soon enough, with the first sip, Francie was on to another subject, this time the things she had seen in the cave outside her hospital window earlier that day: animals turning into birds and then into plants, the dray full of the old people that the Tiger had talked about at the end.

Anna left her mother's side and went over to the window. There was, of course, no cave, no dray and no metamorphosing animals, only a bleak cityscape. She was possessed by an overwhelming urge to jump through the glass, although it was several storeys up and an unforgiving Hobart street lay far below.

But Anna had the sudden sense, that sense you have in dreams, that if she leapt through the window she would not fall to her death but rather that her fall would gently arc into a powerful swoop, and she would find herself flying up Campbell Street, past the marvellous old synagogue in all its mystical Egyptian revival splendour, built by the freed Jewish convicts as if to say both that this island of Van Diemen's Land was their Egypt and that it was not, that it was also freedom.

She would fly over it, not at height, her flying was not so assured, but a metre or two off the ground, flying at a joyful, somewhat terrifying velocity as she glided here and there, her turning controlled by the slightest lean of her shoulders or minutest movement of an outstretched leg in the way she had known in her dreams as a child, a matter of simultaneous stillness and movement; of, in other words, the most perfect balance, all held in control by absolute concentration, an intense focusing on the subtlest of the body's actions, one false movement and the magic ends in the most cataclysmic fall.

But if Anna just believed in the powers of flight a little longer, very soon she would be where she would need to be, which is to say a place of quiet and green, of reverie, perhaps transcendence—

12

But *first* we need to get some details straight, Terzo was saying, and what their younger brother Terzo said normally more or less prevailed as the family view, not Anna's daydreams or Tommy's thoughts but Terzo's will, uttered with his inescapable certainty that Anna now heard fill the ward behind her, so sweetly modulated, robbed of anything stray or unnecessary to its purpose, monotonal as a closing door.

She was suddenly tumbling and falling, she had lost all her powers, and when she turned around from the window to the treacly sound of her brother's voice, it was to hear Terzo speaking to Tommy as if he too were one more of his gullible clients. In the elegance of his Italian suit, the studied casualness of his tieless shirt, with his glittering eyes set in a face too weak for such intensity, Terzo stood in contrast to Tommy with his baggy work jeans, his torn polar fleece top, what Anna always thought of as his butcher's face, somehow fleshy and fallen. She went to raise her hand in greeting to her brothers but dropped it almost as soon as she had lifted it, so that Terzo and Tommy might not notice what Francie had.

The summer was endless in Tasmania that year. None of the normal rules held. There were no spring rains no summer rains. Each day was hot or hotter than the last. For all that though, it was not a bright or happy summer. Out in the island's wildlands there were dry lightning storms that lasted days, thousands upon thousands of lightning strikes igniting small fires everywhere. The rainforests, once wet mystical worlds, were now dry struggling woodlands, and the fires took, and the fires grew; soon, the fires were the only news; they came closer or they drifted away, they advanced or they halted; the point was that wherever they were they continued to inexorably grow and with them the infernal, oppressive smoke, the cinder storms, the reign of ash, and the island's capital filled with the displaced listlessly waiting for the fires to end so that they might return to their homes and their lives.

And yet life itself seemed on hold.

There was a great waiting though for what no one knew. There was an edge and a tension as week after week the fires slowly reduced the ancient forests, the exquisite heathlands and alpine gardens of the island's west and highlands into the ash that Anna, when home seeing her mother, woke each morning to find speckling her Airbnb bed sheet, the fires that rained on the island's old city tiny carbonised fragments of ancient fern and myrtle leaf, perfect negatives that on her touching vanished into a sooty smear, and all that remained of the thousand-year-old King Billy pines and ancient grass trees, the pencil pine groves, the stands of pandani and richea, the great regnans along with the button grass plains and the tiny rare mountain orchids, all that was left of so many sacred worlds was Anna's soot-stained bed sheet.

The smoke had turned the air a tobacco brown, the blinding brilliance of the island's blue skies glimpsed only when the winds blew a small hole in the pall that sat over much of the island. The smoke never seemed to lift and on the worst days reduced everyone's horizon to a few hundred yards and enclosed the world in a way that felt claustrophobic. The sun stumbled into each day a guilty party, a violent red ball, indistinct in outline, shuddering through the haze as if hungover, while in the ochry light smoke smothered every street and the smoke filled every room, the smoke sullied every drink and every meal; the acrid, tarry, sulphurous smoke that burnt the back of every throat and filled every mouth and nose blocking out the warm gentle smells of summer. It was like living with a chronically sick smoker except the smoker was the world and everyone was trapped in its fouled and collapsing lungs.

14

And that Wednesday afternoon, not even an hour earlier, it was this same smoke that burnt Anna's throat and made her cough while she was driving into the Argyle Street car park opposite the Royal Hobart Hospital. On raising her left hand to cover her mouth something seemed strange. She had the odd thought that one of her fingers was missing. It was such an odd thought that she immediately dropped both it and her hand.

As she turned onto the fourth-storey ramp, she brought her left hand to the top of the steering wheel. Once more it seemed not quite right. She glanced down. It wasn't quite right. She saw her thumb and counted three fingers. She swung the wheel around and then swung it back. This time she saw a finger was definitely not where a finger should be and where it should be, next to the little finger, there was, to be precise about it, thought Anna, well, precisely nothing.

She twisted her head around, stealing looks here and there in the car park's crepuscular light, hoping perhaps to see the lost finger leap up. She looked at the hire car's dash as if it might have fallen there. She ran her remaining fingers through the cup holder console but felt only grit and hire car papers. Several times she glanced down at the seat between her legs, and finally the floor.

And realising that this quixotic quest was ridiculous, because you don't just lose a finger like a key or a phone, she jerked her hand—now at nine o'clock on the steering wheel—to twelve o'clock, dragging the wheel back around and nearly driving into an oncoming car as she did so. The other driver beeped, she braked, swerved, halted, and raising a shaking hand to her forehead she felt not relief but a surge of horror.

Between her little finger and her middle finger, where her ring finger had once connected to her hand, there was now a diffuse light, a blurring of the knuckle joint, the effect not unlike the photoshopping of problematic faces, hips, thighs, wrinkles and sundry deformities, with some truth or other blurred out of the picture.

And so too now, it seemed, one of her fingers.

She stared closely at her hand for a good minute. It wasn't a strange illusion or delusion. There was—it was undeniable—no ring finger. She wiggled her thumb and three remaining fingers. They seemed fine, doing the finger things fingers do. There was no pain. There was no immediate sense of ache or loss.

There was just a vanishing.

15

Anna dropped her hand and put the odd event down to the exhaustion she was feeling. Her day had begun with Tommy waking her at two in the morning with a phone call to say Francie had taken a bad turn and had been rushed by ambulance to the Royal Hobart Hospital. It was irritating to say the least, thought Anna, because there was no end to Francie's bad turns which, in hindsight, were never really as bad as Tommy made out.

Tommy's frequent updates on their mother's health sometimes bordered, Anna felt, on the ludicrous. She and Terzo even had a running joke that Tommy had called to say he was very worried about Francie eating/talking/breathing. He seemed to feel it was his duty to keep his siblings abreast of their mother's many infirmities as though they constituted some evidence of a major breakdown in her health.

It was true that there had been a few problems in recent times but each had, after a while, resolved itself. Some years before, Francie had started behaving strangely and her doctor diagnosed dementia. Her walking grew odd, a bizarre half-lollop, half-stagger—like a horse on a bad trip, as Terzo said—and the doctor diagnosed Parkinson's. When she collapsed and was rushed to hospital it was discovered that it was neither dementia nor Parkinson's but rather something else altogether, that she had fluid on the brain, that it was a condition called hydrocephalus, and that it could be relieved by putting an internal shunt up through the back of her neck into her brain, draining the excess fluid into her stomach.

The procedure, frightening as it sounded, proved a success. The oddities of gait and confusions of personality disappeared and, re-emerging into her old self, Francie returned to her life and home and they, her three children, to theirs.

In Anna and Terzo's case, the children who had left the island long ago, that meant phoning their mother more regularly and flying in to see Francie for a day or two every few months. For Tommy, who never left, who was a failing artist and occasional labourer and crayfishing deckie, who, to be frank, Anna thought in her crueller moments, had never really done anything, it did mean a little more. But then Tommy had more time to do more: time to help out with small things— doctors' visits, cooking, shopping, driving Francie to meet her old friends for afternoon tea.

A year passed, and another and another, and three years after the hydrocephalus operation Francie was diagnosed with a slow-developing form of cancer, low grade non-Hodgkin lymphoma. She embarked on a mild course of chemotherapy and at its end, amazingly, went into remission. Francie was, as she herself said, the fittest old corpse in Christendom.

16

And in this way, as if everything had somehow returned to normal, as though tomorrow could never be so very different from today, as if this slow accumulation of ailments and pattern of declining health was of no consequence, almost five years passed, and in those years Anna felt she accomplished so many things she had long wished for.

She had stumbled into the design of Durand House after one of her architectural firm's senior partners died.

The resulting building—a sickle-shaped, steel-spined structure wistfully cantilevered out over a Blue Mountains cliff, a holiday home for the well-known retailer Tony Durand—was hailed as a triumph. Along with a measure of excited architectural babble, it won several national prizes and later a global award for design. But it was for Anna no more or less than making a building from a childhood memory of a eucalyptus leaf.

In no small part because of that success, she was made a partner in the firm. And she met Meg, who worked as a project manager with the construction company that had built Durand House. Anna had seen her around their office, a professional woman to the point of anonymity, then one weekend bumped into her in a café. Meg was wearing yoga pants, dark hair in a top knot that accentuated her cheekbones and her smile. She sat with one leg casually tucked under the other, revealing a strong calf. Sit next to me, she said.

So it began.

17

Some days when they met after work the imprint of the construction helmet's plastic lining was still clear on Meg's forehead, her headband of industry, as Meg called it. Meg didn't care less.

My days are Annie days and non–Annie days and only Annie days are real, Meg might text. The rest never really happen. Every time you go away you come home to a younger woman.

When you're not here I'm not anywhere, Anna might reply.

Dice regrets, Meg would come back, add kale, knead, let gin rise and leave worries to ferment out. At such times Anna found herself reduced to texting emojis of hearts.

Anna felt that in Meg she had found someone with whom she could happily grow old. Anna's son, Gus, was twenty-two, growing up and as Meg would say, *away*, though most of his flight seemed to be into cyberspace in his bedroom. In those years Anna didn't think too much about Gus, or, for that matter, her mother. When she did it was not as her mother was but as a slightly older image of herself, successful, independent, forging her own life her own way, meeting adversity and overcoming it as no doubt, Anna thought, her son similarly thought of her.

And so Tommy annoyed her when he would call or text after the latest fall, crisis, hospitalisation, the most recent domestic drama—evidence of a small fire when she had left a tea towel on a toaster, rotting food found in the fridge, and so on and so forth—matters that were always resolved by Tommy agreeing to sort them out, and Tommy subsequently never really sorting anything out because why else would Anna always end up asking her PA to book yet another flight home?

Tommy was, she felt, almost always overly dramatic

about Francie's latest problems, worried that their mother was somehow or another reaching a critical pass, convinced that these events masked a more fundamental decline. Such was her belief though in the ongoing vitality and good health of their mother—a woman who, as Terzo used to say, could survive a direct nuclear attack—that whenever Tommy contacted her she chastened him for panicking. She was perhaps a little harsh on Tommy. But *really*?

18

Which was why when Tommy rang at two that morning she had told him that their mother was good for another decade or two yet, hung up, switched her phone to silent, lay back down on her bed for just a moment and then there was a voice message from Tommy saying that Francie had had a fall in the hospital trying to get to the toilet. He was there with her at the hospital, things weren't exactly right, they were doing a brain scan at nine. The doctors had asked to meet with the family at four-thirty that afternoon. Terzo was flying in from Brisbane for the meeting.

She checked the time. It was seven o'clock. Because of the early hour she had to reschedule her meetings for the day herself, and book a flight for midday herself, all of which was annoying enough, and then, because of the bushfire smoke blanketing southern Tasmania, her flight was delayed four hours. She texted Tommy several times, but Tommy, as was his way, didn't reply. She drifted into her social media. An article on herbal remedies for anxiety. On new bathroom trends. On a town about to run dry that had all its remaining water granted to a coal mining company. Posts of friends travelling. Whitegoods clothes shoes cosmetics conspiracies a farmer tweeting how kangaroos kept lying down in his front garden and dying drought is a bushfire in slow motion, he wrote. Like share update friend subscribe. There was so much noise. Tommy texted that a cruise ship was playing the *Love Boat* theme so loudly with its foghorns that in the hospital no one could hear their own thoughts.

19

The three children awkwardly shared the small space in their mother's single-bed hospital room, taking it in turns to sit in the blue vinyl chair next to the bed to talk with Francie, while the other two whispered at the bed's end. When Anna's turn came, she reached across with her right hand to her mother's fingers, curling her left on the splitting vinyl of the armrest to better obscure her newly discovered deficiency. Francie tried to follow both the conversation of the sitter and the whispering of the two standing and soon enough, exhausted from the effort, fell asleep.

It was late in the afternoon when two doctors arrived and with soft voices introduced themselves. Beneath the bright neon, Mr Ram, the neurosurgeon, quietly drew the family around to one side of the bed. Mr Ram was tall and wore a turban and had an odour that Anna associated with professionals, a neutral deodorant smell. He told them there was the fluid from the hydroceph-alus, which was safely under control with the shunt dispersing it, but now on the front left of the brain there was a small haemorrhage. Mr Ram rapped his turban with his knuckles and smiled as if to signal this was not something that needed to be worried about. Our brains, he said, like all motors, get a little loose over time.

The family nervously smiled back. Mr Ram tapped the side of his nose with a finger as if he had somehow secured a slightly illicit deal built on an unspoken complicity.

Behind their small circle Anna could see her mother buttressed into an upright position by several pillows, Adam's apple rising and dropping in her wasted throat as she slept, ceaselessly swallowing, as they made decisions that would determine her fate. She momentarily awoke, as if startled—eyelids red and inflamed, like wounds out of which sickly eyeballs protruded unnaturally, overly large, bloodshot and yellowed, with cloudy irises—and almost as quickly fell back to sleep.

At eighty-six years of age, Mr Ram continued, there would be enough space in the cavity between the age-shrunken brain and the skull for a small bleed—such as their mother had experienced—to accumulate and for it not to be felt as pressure, or as pain, or for any really noticeable long-term effect on their mother's faculties. While there might be some mental impairment it would likely be short term, and the body would slowly reabsorb the blood the way it did after a bad bruising. He was explaining to the family that he felt it far wiser after a brain haemorrhage at Francie's age to manage the problem without recourse to surgery when he was interrupted by a rasping voice.

Did me good, Francie croaked from her bed, shocking everyone. The family turned awkwardly to face their ailing mother who, they had assumed, was sleeping. Haven't had such a damaging rush of blood to the head since I met your father, she said.

And, of all things, she winked at them.

20

As they nervously laughed Francie went to smile back. But the haemorrhage must have affected her control of her mouth. She could raise only one side of her upper lip, revealing a few crooked yellow teeth unnaturally long where the gums had pulled back, giving the effect of a skull sneering. Their mother's cheeky words and cheery gesture were so at odds with this dreadful appearance that it seemed grotesque. Anna had the momentary impression that she was seeing a corpse talk. But as Francie had just made clear she was very much alive in that wretched body.

Tommy stepped forward and, reaching down, put his arms beneath their mother, lifted her face to his and held it there, and without any sense of shame or embarrassment but with the greatest tenderness whispered, Mum! Oh, Mum! as he rocked that old raddled flesh as if it were his own newly born.

And though Anna found Tommy's spontaneous gesture undignified, even an affront to their mother's dignity, somehow, with Francie's wink and Tommy's embrace it felt that they had been made complicit in their mother's old age and her body's collapse, as if the hydrocephalus and the cancer and now the haemorrhage and all her mother's woes had also become theirs.

Anna felt not pity but revulsion bordering on a strange fear. She could deal with death, or she could deal with life, but her mother's toggling between the two was, for her—a woman of plans built and timetables agreed and spreadsheets obeyed: a person, it could be said, in short, of certainty—an unexpected and irritating resistance to the natural flow of things, evidence of little more than an erratic and selfish spirit.

The confusion of finding not her mother in that hospital bed but a terribly sick animal who refused to stop being human was at some deep level unacceptable to Anna. Yes, that was it. An animal, a sick animal.

She needed to get away from it, lest it infect her with its disease.

In the deepest part of Anna's being, she was thinking that it might be simpler and altogether less difficult if the woman lying in that bed who happened to be her mother was dead. Or, at the least, at the best, that she would agree to die, rather than winking and insisting on staying alive.

And then, shocked at her most private thoughts, Anna wondered if she lacked something other people took for granted, some necessary humanity or compassion or empathy. Perhaps something was wrong with her. Perhaps she was wicked. Perhaps this was why her marriage had failed, why her son was the way he was. She could not say. Her mind was a jungle. She horrified herself.

At that moment her mother's weary, awful eyes caught hers and she felt captured by that face so much like her own—except so lined, so decayed. Anna shuddered with such a strange confusion of feelings that Tommy, looking up, let Francie go and stepping away from the bed grabbed her wrist and, squeezing it, whispered, I know! I know!

Anna was overwhelmed with the greatest guilt because it did not seem possible to love someone and want them dead at the same time. How could she think such horrible things? And precisely because of her shame she saw that henceforth she would have to devote her very being to keeping her mother alive. She heard herself involuntarily moan.

I know! I know! Tommy babbled again.

But what did Tommy know? Did Tommy know that she wanted their mother dead? Did Tommy know that was why she had now to commit to keeping her alive? Was he, too, as much a hypocrite as her?

She looked at him and these thoughts angered her, and Tommy angered her because she felt them and she felt them very deeply but she could not say them. She would not say them and she understood she must never again even think such terrible things. Bringing her hand up she pushed her brother's away. Perhaps he was just a fucking idiot, Anna thought. It was possible. Anything was possible.

21

And suddenly aware of her missing finger she dropped her hand as quickly as she had raised it. Mr Ram was now speaking of how in some ways the brain haemorrhage would have positive outcomes. Medication for her heart, her blood pressure, her constipation, her depression, and her fluid retention had all been *recalibrated*, and she would now go from fourteen pills a day to nine.

Nine, Francie said from her bed. Now nine *is* good.

Mr Ram smiled. He was hopeful that over time they could reduce the number of pills to six. And six was a magical number! he told them. Too many daily pills only created further complications, and complications on complications with side effects multiplying madly, and he went so far as to cite both studies and his own experience in this regard.

Isn't that right, Frances? he asked, turning to the patient. But the old woman who had for a moment seemed rejuvenated by her plight only made a slight whistling noise with her throat in reply, having fallen asleep so quickly that no one had noticed.

The family nodded, the family murmured, the family made as if they understood all this and everything else, though discussing it after in the hospital corridor they had to admit they didn't understand it entirely or exactly, or, for that matter, really understand it at all.

22

All three were exhausted and agreed to meet again the next morning at the hospital. Anna was finally able to check into her apartment. Once inside, she had the necessary solitude to minutely examine the improbable fact of her missing finger.

She held her hand up close to her eyes, examining the space where the finger should be, the slightly blurred boundary where it had once joined with her hand, and wiggled her remaining fingers. It had to be admitted it didn't really cause her any problem. Even when she shook her hand there was no pain. And although her hand wasn't quite as functional with three fingers as it had been with four it worked well enough, and she had never been one to fuss about herself.

She did worry though that it might be a sign of cancer because at her age everything—every bruise, wheeze, bump and lump—was read by her as a premonition, a precursor, a symptom and first sign of a fatal tumour. But when she thought about it a cancer is an addition, a growth, whereas a missing finger is a reduction, a subtraction—an absence. So it could not be cancer though what it was or might mean was puzzling.

Anna put her reading glasses on. She googled *vanished fingers*. Nothing. Nothing? She switched on every light. She held her hand up to the brightest, she held it up to the window, she held it under the bedside lamp, she brought it towards her and took it away, as though the absence would finally prove merely a focusing error of her wretched ageing eyes.

She took her glasses off and once more held the offending extremity centimetres from her eyes. She turned it this way and that. She examined it from every angle, she touched, smelt and finally licked the strangely amorphous stump that wasn't quite there and wasn't quite not there. The stump was soft and tasted of nothing. Her tongue slightly tickled, but when she experimented her tongue also tickled if she touched it on her thumb, her palm, her wrist.

Really, the new hand felt normal, no different from her old hand. It was impossible to say why she felt so oddly about it, thought Anna. It was her hand, after all. Except somehow, looking at it, in a way she had no words to describe, it no longer was.

TWO

1

The missed text from Tommy was timestamped 4.07 am—

Mum had 2nd brain harmony at midfnight much worse than first seems v serious. Tx

Anna checked the time. It was six-something. At the hospital she found Francie in the ICU ward, unconscious, almost unrecognisable, one side of her face drooping as if deboned, breathing tube snaking into her slack mouth, aged a decade overnight.

After two hours of mute terror, Anna was relieved to see a young registrar walk in. She stayed only a minute, mumbling about hypoxia and neurological problems, and how she would call Mr Ram immediately. An hour later she returned with Mr Ram. Perhaps more out of pity than for any diagnostic purpose, or, simply to buy time to think, he put his hand on Francie's forehead.

Head cast down, he stood lost in his own thoughts. His previous day's optimism had abandoned him.

2

Finally he took his hand away and looked up. He spoke with an immense weariness. He told them he could operate. He could drill a hole through the skull to drain the blood, allowing the brain to decompress. But the prognosis was very far from ideal.

Very far? Tommy asked.

The risks were not inconsiderable, Mr Ram said. At their mother's age they may well be insurmountable.

Terzo bluntly asked what that meant.

Mr Ram replied that it *meant* her brain might be badly affected.

There was a long silence during which Mr Ram's cheeks twitched.

It *meant*, Mr Ram said, that she might die. Whilst operating. It *meant* that if she survived the operation she might lose the ability to speak, or, worse, the reduction of the mind to a near-vegetative state. Would their mother want that? He spoke of how they had *a choice*. He spoke of how the final days of a loved one could be a good time for a family. He spoke of how he had seen it many times. *He spoke he spoke he asked* had she left an advanced care directive?

No one replied.

Did they know what their mother's wishes were, Mr Ram asked.

They had no idea. Terzo and Anna turned to Tommy. After all, Tommy talked with Francie a lot. He even said he *liked* talking with her.

Tommy's answer was less than helpful.

When she was sick, Tommy said, she would say let me die. But when she was well—well, she would say just patch me up and keep me going.

Mr Ram continued . . . peg feeding . . . multiple-organ failure . . . respect . . . dignity . . . *he spoke he spoke he spoke* abruptly he stopped.

He wince-smiled.

He said he would leave them to make their decision, nodded, and left the ward.

3

The three children stood at a short distance from Francie's bed, silent. No one had ever told them that at the end there was a choice and it is not the dying who make it.

Dignity, Terzo finally whispered as if to himself, that's what Francie wants.

Tommy seemed to mumble some agreement but he was unable to finish his sentence. As if uncertain what *dignity* meant.

Terzo, who was uncertain about little, said the real

question was of contempt versus respect: should their mother die wretchedly or die peacefully? The doctors seemed to be of the opinion, one, that Francie was ready to die and, two, that to medically intervene would only prolong the agony of her dying.

Yet listening, Anna said she felt that *they* were not ready. *They* were not prepared in any sense. *They* were still their mother's children. Why could their mother not decide for them? Anna could not.

As Terzo continued talking of respect she said nothing, waiting for the moment when she might leave.

When Mr Ram came back, as Terzo told him that the family saw no point in proceeding with the operation, she watched Tommy step up to the bed, lean down, whisper to their mother how much he loved her, and gently kiss Francie on her forehead. Her left arm rose up from the bed until it was a little higher than her face, a simulacrum of an embrace for her boy. And as Tommy kissed her it stayed hovering in mid-air, skin hanging from its bones, shuddering with a slight tremor and a great emotion.

4

Not knowing what else to do, they went to lunch. The restaurant—chosen by Terzo, the family gourmand—comprised the same bench tables as Baku or Berlin's finest; the same bearded waiters and the same cant as

Seattle or Santiago about how their restaurant was different—their *philosophy* was sharing plates, had they ever had sharing plates?—the same incongruous ingredients confettied with some edible Instagrammable bling, guaranteed as worthy by the same smug boasts of the local provenance of everything from the seventies slipware to the silver beet. In another age such dishes would have been Dadaist jokes. Seaweed smoked with ice-cream, or was it, Terzo asked, smoke ice-creamed with seaweed?

Anna and Terzo were joined by an unspoken guilt: in recent years they had not been there for their mother, a guilt that now felt an almost impossible weight, knowing she was soon to die. Anna and Terzo both had what people call comforts: a little money, a little power. By the standards of the real rich, pitiful; by the metrics of the truly powerful, negligible, even laughable. But still: money and power. And they were accustomed to acting on the world and not allowing the world to act on them.

And yet what was any of it worth if it could not help their mother?

That burden had fallen on their eldest brother, Tommy. But as they did not see Tommy as their equal because Tommy had no money and no power, and, even more strangely, seemed to have no particular interest in either, Tommy had in some indefinable way shamed his siblings.

And yet, he, the lesser one, with all his disadvantages, had done for their mother everything that they had not.

And this offended their sense of their power and wealth. And perhaps it was this offence, which was also an unspoken anger, which explains why—when Tommy agreed with Terzo, how all things considered, terrible as it was, maybe it was for the best to let Francie die—everything changed.

5

Terzo's fork, mid-air with something intricate, artisanal and garlanded finely balanced upon it, froze. His fingers were long white skinny things. Other than the prominence of the bulging joints, which gave them the profile of bamboo, his hands were soft and unformed like those of a marsupial.

Never! he said. He would *Never. Say. Anything. Of. The. Sort.*

Terzo and Anna—who had so adroitly invested their money and who had treated their bodies as their most precious investment of all, exercising, maintaining, preserving and enhancing them with all that their money could buy—had resisted time and illness, so slowing their own ageing, so postponing their own deaths, that, on being presented with Tommy's summary of what they had previously agreed about their mother, felt offended.

Terzo's slate platter dully clanked as he laid his fork down.

What he *had* said, said Terzo, was that *a humane effort* must be made.

Put that way it somehow sounded noble and right to Anna—as if it were a necessary truth. How could Tommy think otherwise?

Terzo said Tommy made it sound a death sentence. As though they had no control over such things.

Was that the real insult, Anna sometimes later wondered—*that they might have lost control?* As Terzo ate all of the beetroot hummus without noticing, Anna, having previously agreed with Terzo that the operation was a pointless cruelty and nothing more could be done, now understood it was necessary to fight to regain control.

And if that meant the operation, Terzo said, picking at his teeth with a manicured thumb nail, then the operation it must be.

Tommy, however, seemed unable to appreciate that the family line had swung 180 degrees. He said that by allowing the operation and the horrors that might flow from it weren't they not so much extending Francie's life as prolonging her death into a living hell? Or, worse, robbing her of a few precious final weeks for a death on the operating table?

It wasn't a question of how long, Anna pointed out to Tommy, but rather a question of fighting this thing with all the resources they could muster as a family.

Terzo agreed. His mother was not going to die alone.

His mother? Tommy said.

Terzo was off quoting people. You live as you die, alone, he said. Chekhov. To die like a dog, alone. Kafka.

So what was this, asked Tommy. TEDfucktalk? When did Terzo ever open a book? Terzo didn't know what those people wrote. He didn't know those people. No. Tommy did not agree. He did not think Francie would just be pegging it out on her lonesome. He would be there. He knew that much. He would be there and she would not be alone. What was Terzo's real fear? Death? Or being alone? Tommy understood his own life might be a failure. Yes. Still: a life lived. Yes. Y-y-yes. He was not alone and nor would Francie be alone.

The thing is, Tommy, Anna said, seeking to ignore Tommy, to rein him in and return the conversation to where she and Terzo wanted it. They knew *people*. And even if they didn't know the people they needed, they knew other people who knew them.

Terzo said that was the important thing, the only thing, to work *in favour of life*.

It was like tag-team wrestling. Only Tommy had no one to tag and he was soon enough quiet and quiescent. Such conversations became to Anna about dignity—dignity and the deformations of dignity, dignity and the need to keep dignity free from the dangerous filth of family love. Tommy, viewed in this light, was contaminating, that most bourgeois of embarrassments: the lower-class relative. And though Tommy never hurt Anna, she would hurt him, and she would hate Tommy for revealing that aspect of herself to them both.

In recent years Tommy inclined to silence around his brother and sister, the voluble runs of angry language and rickety flights of rocketing thoughts of his younger years now only occasionally heard and easily enough extinguished.

To keep Francie alive, Anna continued.

But Tommy's head had long before dropped. He said nothing.

And from having only a few hours earlier been convinced that their mother would die, the family had somehow abruptly resolved that, above all things, Francie must now live.

6

After telling the surgeon one thing in the morning, Terzo informed him of the opposite in the afternoon. The family, having thought on it all, had concluded that if the only hope of their mother living, no matter how slim, was surgery, then surgery it had to be.

Mr Ram brought his hands together in front of his chin and tapped the side of his nose with a finger. He said if that was their wish there could be no waiting: their mother would go to theatre immediately.

Treacly hours passed. Finally Mr Ram reappeared.

Their mother was alive.

She was still alive the next day, and she was still alive the day after that. Slowly it became clear that something almost miraculous was happening—Francie was healing and there were no complications. After four days the breathing tube came out. After a week their mother, if frail and easily tired, was talking. Her facial droop was far less pronounced. Mr Ram was pleased. They were astonished.

And when after two weeks she seemed back to her old self and in some ways better, face restored and her spirits particularly high, the physios declared themselves amazed and they could all only agree: Terzo's newly found determination that Francie live had not been misplaced.

7

Terzo began talking of Francie moving out of the hospital and back into the family home. It was simply a case, as Terzo put it, of everyone making an *effort*.

By *effort*, Anna understood that Terzo really meant more money, because although each of them loved Francie in their own way, she and Terzo were also busy successful people whose busy successful lives didn't allow that love to be shown as time with their mother. To ensure that Francie continued with her life so that they might continue with theirs they would, as Terzo now outlined, keep buying her life with all the expertise and resources they could afford using all the influence and connections they most surely had to ensure the best care possible.

And in this way a new equilibrium would be established, a tolerable pattern in which life could once more go on seeming possible, a new life in which they each could return to their old lives.

Tommy, on the other hand, who had devoted much of his life to their mother but who had neither money nor influence to make the effort of which Terzo spoke, stopped stammering and fell silent.

And that was that.

8

Anna's first day back home in Sydney passed much as any other day except that she no longer had her finger. But as the finger's absence caused no pain nor created any great difficulties she ignored it. And besides, to draw attention to a missing finger when her mother was so ill, when Gus needed attention, when her work was more maddening than ever, seemed to Anna, well, overdone. Indulgent, even selfish.

Yet in spite of not wanting people to notice she began to grow irritated when no one did. Thursday came and went and no one at work said anything.

Friday was the same. By the following Tuesday night, when Gus refused yet again to leave his bedroom for a chicken biryani—his favourite—which she had cooked specially for him, she felt more than miffed; by Thursday, when still nobody had said a word, she was more than annoyed; and after Gus again didn't bother joining her for dinner but had a pizza delivered later in the evening she was enraged.

The next evening she was so angry that when she met Meg for a drink after work she almost immediately went on a rant about the spurned biryani before thrusting her hand up into Meg's face and asking her what she thought.

Meg tucked one leg under the other, and said that Gus was twenty-five, he seemed to have no visible means of support other than his mother, and perhaps it was time he moved out and got a job.

It wasn't about Gus, Anna said, but this!—and she waved her hand furiously—my hand, Meg! My *fucking* hand!

9

Meg, whose vanity meant she didn't wear her prescription glasses in social situations, straightened her legs and sat up, craning her head so far forward that Anna could smell her shampoo. She stared closely until, finally, she asked what sort of ring it was.

Only after Anna told Meg to count her fingers did the truth, after a fashion, dawn. Meg told Anna that she never knew Anna only had three fingers. Anna explained to Meg that she never *only* had three fingers, that *only* having three fingers was a very recent thing, that she always *only* had four fingers, like Meg, four fingers and a thumb, like the entire rest of the world, and then—*well*, it was hard to explain.

But a finger had gone missing? Meg asked.

Yes, she knew, *she knew*; the thing is now she had three fingers and she didn't know what had happened to the fourth and that was the worst of it, not losing the finger, which, she confessed, had proved less traumatic than you might think. No, it was the strangeness of its disappearance, the way it had vanished without accident or pain, the way she had no memory of its vanishing, *that* was what was traumatic. The way something is until it isn't. Her finger was there as you assume fingers are, more or less, for life, and then, when she looked, Anna said, well . . .

Well? Meg said.

Well, it wasn't.

10

Meg ordered two double martinis. She said she had an uncle who could cure warts just by looking at them. Explain that.

Anna replied that she couldn't. Meg was silent. Anna looked at her phone—a waterfall of faces that were and were not in her life, friends, workmates, celebrities, an ex-boyfriend—six years older than Anna with a thirty-something woman and a new baby—all falling, so many meaningless droplets briefly lit before going dark before returning remarried, single, partnered, ever triumphal, while half of Greenland's surface ice sheet melted, France had its hottest day on record, a tiny Australian marsupial rat was the first species to be wiped out by climate change and the last Sumatran rhinoceros died.

In a voice that seemed both fearful and angry Anna heard Meg ask how the hell such a thing had happened. She looked up from her phone and told Meg the truth, which was that it hadn't really happened at all. Her finger was there until in the Argyle Street car park it wasn't.

Meg wondered if the shock of her mother's illness had undone Anna's mind. Maybe she didn't remember what had happened. But *something* must have happened.

Meg was staring at her as if she were a ghost, or mad, or both, a mad ghost, thought Anna, anyone but her dear friend. Meg said Anna had to go to a doctor. She needed help.

Anna replied that help was pointless, that it was healed, that, in fact, there never was any wound, strange as it may sound, or pain, or blood, or whatever, nothing *medical*, so there wasn't anything a doctor could do other than have her locked up. And she wasn't really up for that. Not yet. In any case, she was well on the way to being reconciled to having only three fingers on one hand. And besides, what could be done? Getting old was simply about losing so many things: hearing, teeth, sight, sense, and now, she guessed, body parts.

Perhaps it wasn't that strange.

Meg said that Anna wasn't old, that she was fifty-nine and that fifty-nine wasn't old at all.

Fifty-six, Anna curtly corrected her friend.

Fifty-six wasn't so old either, Meg said. It certainly wasn't old enough to think some silent leprosy was okay.

Anna asked Meg if she thought it might be a weird menopause thing? She had thought she was through all that, but, maybe it was, like, you know, some late hormonal thing?

Meg, who had turned forty-three two weeks before, said maybe, she wouldn't know, they say it affected every woman differently, but she'd never heard of pieces of women falling off because of menopause. I mean, she went on, that's completely crazy. Did she think it might be early onset dementia?

Anna told Meg to fuck off.

Fuck off you, Meg replied. Holding up a hand in which the middle fingers were tucked into her palm, she pretended to wave it at someone in the mid distance. Five beers here! Her grandfather had been a log truck driver, Meg said. He called it the sawmiller's shout.

Anna told Meg that wasn't funny. Meg asked if it hurt and when she said it didn't Meg said that's okay then.

It's not okay! Anna heard herself suddenly yell. It's gone!

11

Meg looked down at her friend's three-fingered hand. Anna looked down. They were both looking and looking but for the life of them they couldn't work out what it was they weren't seeing.

12

For a time, by placing it on her lap, holding it under tables, putting it in a pocket, or by bunching her hand in a way that made the absence harder to spot Anna was able to hide it from the gaze of others. *For a time*. But then she forgot and forgot again, and people still said nothing. Did they really see nothing? Or did they see something and place no more weight on it than they might a webbed toe, a long chin, a broken nose?

In any case, amidst the pressures of work compounded by her more frequent visits to Tasmania to see her mother, Anna often forgot about her finger altogether. The Hobart hospital corridors gradually became as familiar to her as the street on which she lived—the neon-lit tunnels along which she made her way through the befuddled odours of disinfectant and death, past cleaning trolleys with their chipped enamelled metal rings dangling bright burnt orange plastic bags, the shark-mouthed sharps boxes, hand-sanitising stations, silent gurneys and gossipy ward stations, amidst a clustering chaos of signs signalling to Anna only her own growing confusion.

And as familiar as these sights was Francie's inevitable greeting when Anna arrived and asked her mother how she was. Francie was almost always sitting up, wearing over her nightie a red woollen cardigan Anna had bought her, a magenta red that made her face seem older and paler, but also somehow . . . *jubilant*. Francie would slowly look up, stare and, no matter her health, on realising who it was, break into a wide smile and give her joyful cry: All the better for seeing you, girl! *Now*—sit here and tell me all your stories.

13

Every visit began with Francie delighted and never morbid; talking not of herself but of others. For their pains and pleasures were Francie's and weighed against them hers were of no consequence. Perhaps, as Terzo said, it was how she saw the world. But by seeing the world that way that was the way the world came to her.

Tommy pointed out that the only thing that would have surprised their mother about her fate was if it had involved solitude. She understood herself only as existing through others, whether it was the nurses and patients who were so much the warp and weft of her daily life, or the stories of her friends and children. Even in her delusions and nightmares, even in her dreams, when the old people came calling for her on the dray she was never alone.

Was that the real distinction between the past and the present, Anna wondered sometimes. Between the world her mother had grown up in, materially poor but spiritually rich, and the world in which she, her daughter, now lived: her mother never alone while she often felt that she lived in a perfect hell of solitude.

Francie had come of age in a world where the self—its problems, its needs, its desires and its vanities—was not accorded the primacy of time or the dignity of reflection for people of her lowly class. All that was dismissed as so many eccentricities and indulgences, something alien, irredeemably comic. Possibly American. Most likely.

As a woman, as the daughter of poor people, Francie had learnt to live through other people—husbands, children, friends, extended family, acquaintances. For that enforced selflessness her mother had paid a terrible price in terms of a professional life, a public life, a private life realising her full possibilities—but equally, it was undeniable, thought Anna: here, now, constantly alive in that world of others, she was allowed this recompense: the only stranger in her life was solitude.

And sitting with her ill mother in that anonymous hospital ward Anna sometimes found herself envying Francie terribly, and she was happy for her, and she was astonished by her. For Francie had paid the price, and she was not alone.

THREE

But all too soon all that had seemed containable by her mother's stoicism, by her humour and her courage, could no longer be contained.

A scheduled move to hospice facilities where there were rehabilitation services to prepare Francie for a return to life outside the hospital kept being postponed. Difficulties began and then began cascading—breathing issues, chest pains, infections, pneumonias, heart problems, the seemingly endless collapses and falls.

Where formerly Francie had always given news of the doctors' good reports and their encouraging words, even when on reflection it seemed those words hadn't really been that good or so encouraging, now she would merely nod when pushed by her children about a doctor's visit, and, if pushed hard, would only say it had been *the normal thing*—more prodding and more questions. ·

Soon there was not one or even many problems but something else, something that wasn't quite a crisis and wasn't quite not a crisis, a depressing and gathering mudslide of complications, and complications on complications; side effects, and side effects of side effects, and all seemingly without end.

2

In spite of the help they were getting for Francie, the three children sensed something in their mother ebbing away as the mounting toll of small events—falls, colds, gastric upsets, tearing skin, ulcerating pressure sores—began taking effect.

Rarely now the jubilant cry of welcome; increasingly —after a long trip, critical work postponed, meetings rearranged, work done too quickly or even slipshodly, conscious of precious time lost and rueing it—Anna would arrive only for Francie to scarcely seem able to register her presence.

Some days it would be as much as Francie was capable of to reach out her hand and place it over Anna's and, unable to speak, nod in a way that suggested her head was too heavy for her neck and drop it back into her pillow. Each visit her face seemed further changed, more harrowed, more lined, more extraordinary as flesh vanished from it. Anna felt she was seeing her mother for the first time, a fierce face with a sharp nose and strong jaw, as if the process of decay was excavating daily a little more of some truth that her daughter had never previously known.

There were always flowers, sometimes too many for the little chest of drawers, and they sat on the floor up against the wall as if it were a shrine.

They made her feel like the Cenotaph on Anzac Day, Francie told Anna on one of the few visits when she still talked. Except, she said, she would rather forget.

3

Still, Francie—as if her hospital bed were her home— would offer her daughter what little she had whenever Anna visited. In a gesture as slow and deliberate as a crane moving a tilt slab across a building site her thin puckered fingers would shudder across the expanse of bedspread with a biscuit saved from her morning tea or the grapes Tommy had brought days before. She would suggest that her daughter should move her chair so she might sit in the sun.

Such a beautiful day, Francie would say. We can share the sun.

That was really all Francie had left, Anna thought. A small patch of light that fell by her bedside. And even that she gladly gave away.

In the past when Anna had visited Francie in her home—which was rarely—there were always fresh cakes or biscuits or bread, things Anna never wanted to eat and would often rudely dismiss, not realising that the offering of food was always something her mother had prepared and baked just for her—the most fundamental gift of hospitality that could be made. Her mother: the most welcoming of hosts. And the most grateful.

And though the family kitchen, with its electric clock that was always losing time, was gone, there remained in the smallness of space that was her hospital bed the same largeness of spirit, the same defiance of what time wrought. Anna would sit in the dusty glare, would eat the dry biscuit or the shrivelled grape, not wanting any of it but as a form of penance for her sin of not adequately reciprocating that love.

And each time she sat in her mother's light she would sense the weight of her guilt transform into the strangest, most welcome lightness and she would feel an unexpected sense of grace take hold.

4

One visit Anna found her mother distressed. With embarrassment Francie explained she had soiled herself but didn't wish to trouble a nurse.

Anna called for help and with a nurse rolled Francie on her side. The smell was awful, sharp with supplements and drugs and drips. The nurse adroitly changed the sheets and set about cleaning Francie. Her mother grimaced from a touch or movement several times but, as if it would be an indignity too far, gave not a word of complaint.

Anna took her mother's hand, a stiff, knobbly thing, crippled and crooked. It was waxy and cold, the old skin like some ancient oiled leather. Francie had little strength, but the tenacity of that grip! Bones and skin clutching her, as if in a blessing or as though it were a message, or both things and much else besides.

5

Holding her mother's hand Anna thought of how when she was a child her mother kept a little bottle of face cream, called Oil of Ulan. The cream was a musk colour, which always put her in mind of old stockings. The Oil of Ulan was the only luxury her mother ever permitted herself. Anna recalled no perfumes or cosmetics. Though her mother liked such things she went without.

Anna found some cream in her handbag and with her good hand slowly worked it into Francie's fingers so that the scent might predominate over a persistent faecal and ammoniacal odour. She worked each of her mother's fingers slowly and gently, marvelling at the leathery skin, the lack of flexibility, the arthritic lumps.

Such ugly old mitts, Francie said. Scare the hair off a hound!

Anna ran her thumb lightly over the back of her

mother's hand and Francie stopped talking as though it were a signal that her daughter was to rub and she to rest, knowing they had this, whatever it was, whatever it meant, mother and daughter who had so often fought in the past, who had for so long been two now knowing a return, however briefly, to being one.

Anna had always dreaded visiting, resenting the time lost, the imposition and difficulties created, and yet now, once there, seated beside her mother, it somehow felt an enormous relief. She would watch over the rolling throat, the crusted skin, the rising and falling chest, the slack mouth, the tremor of chapped lips.

The immense effort living can be.

Anna, who had backed Terzo in not allowing Francie to die, in no small part so she could continue a life free of her mother, now found herself in the odd situation of visiting her more frequently. Every eight or ten weeks somehow became every six weeks and six weeks, imperceptibly, became monthly and soon enough it was every second weekend, until the most precious thing in Anna's life was sitting beside her mother in the hospital ward.

And in that subjugation to something other than herself she felt unexpectedly and strangely free. Everything felt chaos in her life except when she found herself at Francie's bedside where, without complication or confusion, an inexplicable serenity would take hold of her. And in this way, or so it seemed to her, they were allowed to be.

I am so old, Annie, Francie said finally. So old and ugly. And she smiled. Well, at least I have an excuse to be ugly now.

6

While Anna ran a thumb back and forth over the wrinkles of Francie's hand, summer turned to autumn, the Tasmanian fires ended, winter came and went, spring arrived, Australia began burning, and on the ever rarer occasions she thought of her missing finger it seemed silly to worry while Francie, relieved from the obligations of conversations she knew were beyond her, conversations perhaps beyond them both, gazed at the ceiling, her laboured breath the only sound, as Anna alternately gently piled and smoothed soft ridges of her mother's loose, liver-spotted skin.

7

On the days that Francie had the energy to talk she could still be chatty, and Anna would listen as her mother told her of the strange things she had seen. The man in the ward opposite who kept ferrets hidden in his pyjama trousers. The CIA spies who lived in a cave just outside the window, faces blank plates from which noses, ears, lips had slid off so all that remained was a single central eye, watchful and mournful.

Strangely, her mother was not frightened by her visions. Even when she had little strength for anything else she would talk to Anna about the mountain plains outside her window full of fires and sandstorms where, nightly, women queued in one area for abortions and in another for orgies, where fleeing people turned into plants only to perish in flames, and where she passed the time talking with the witch and Constantine.

She observed the madnesses of flesh and soul in the manner of a natural historian finding in them something vaguely absurd and frequently intriguing.

Oh, it's astonishing, Annie, what you see when you look, she would say.

She witnessed the strange sex and medical procedures, observed the ecstasies, the tedium, the anguish, the indifference and the emotion, the flight and the flames, took in a universe of things, without feeling the need to judge it. If it brought on any feeling it seemed to be amusement.

All this was deeply at odds with her harsh Catholic upbringing. The old shibboleths she had repeated through her life vanished: she finally spoke of the world as she found it. The hard woman she had sometimes been, the merciless mother, the priest-fearing penitent who knew the wages of mortal sin were hell: all these ideas of herself vanished and with them there fell away the illusions of the ward along with the prison of her failing body.

What stood revealed?

Perhaps, thought Anna, looking on that frail old woman so vulnerable in her hospital bed, it was Francie's true nature which she saw too late was open, gentle, and loving. Had her mother's temper and hardness served only to hide her immense disappointments and unacknowledged pain? Was that the cost of her enormous unspoken struggle?

For her part, Francie seemed to view that world to which she now daily escaped through her window with a grateful wonder. And like a dream she didn't want it to stop. For if her visions ended she might wake to know the dust and flames where she spent her days had finally consumed not only her but all those she chatted about as if they were dear friends whom she saw daily.

It's a marvellous privilege, she told her daughter. Where else would you get to talk with the witch and Constantine?

8

As Francie's confusions grew so too did the clarity and conviction with which she spoke of them, and Anna would find herself in turn confused, feeling that perhaps the real world was a greater illusion than her mother's wild imaginings. Sometimes Anna found that the only way to make conversation was to believe in Francie's fantasies a little. Just a little.

If none of Francie's delusions shocked her she was

still taken aback when, lifting washing she was returning out of a bag, her mother once more asked what on earth had happened to her finger. Anna told her it was nothing, that it was long ago, a kitchen accident.

And at that moment Francie, not a woman to be put off a line of enquiry when it came to her children, was thankfully diverted by a nurse arriving with her pharmacopeia of daily pills.

9

One day, out of nowhere, as Anna was brushing Francie's hair, Francie asked her about *that* poem, you know, that one about how your parents mess you up?

Her mother had always had such beautiful hair, thick, brunette, almost auburn in colour, and even after she let it go white it had good shape. But now it had grown pitifully thin.

As she kept brushing, Anna replied that yes, she knew it.

Auden? her mother asked.

Larkin, Anna replied. She didn't quote the correct word back to her mother.

Larkin? Yes. Well, Francie said, the poem isn't true. We mess ourselves up. Or perhaps it is worse than that, perhaps we are simply born messed up. Maybe some parents are monsters. But aren't they mostly just us? Aren't we just them?

Sitting up in her bed, she seemed to Anna like a small child eager to do right and please, the small child Anna imagined Francie's father had so loved, basking in the love Francie knew was hers and which flowed from her father unstinted and without measure, so unlike Francie's own resentful mother whose love was poisoned by guilt and the shame visited on her by her husband's family.

She sometimes wondered, Francie continued, if parents' mistake was to make too much of their importance to their children, and their children repeat the same mistake.

10

As the brush passed through her mother's thin hair Anna didn't wish to see the mottled scalp visible beneath its strands and wisps. She brushed as gently as she could, careful where a dark scab crust, yellow-and-blue rimmed, marked the hole that had been bored through her skull. Her mother sat still and silent as a chastened child. For a moment Anna glimpsed how Francie must have suffered with her own mother's madness and rages.

She leant down and whispered into Francie's ear.

I know, her mother said, as if closing a draughty door for them both to be once more warm. I know, girl.

And with that Francie abruptly changed subject, asking when she would be able to recommence physiotherapy, and if she might visit the hospital gym, as the rehabilitation room was known, to do some preparatory work on the exercise bike.

And when Anna reassured Francie that she was sure it would be soon, that the doctors would know, Francie told her that the young doctor had said she was doing well under the circumstances. But, Francie said, he hadn't said the circumstances that she was under. Which were, she guessed, that she wasn't really getting better at all.

Her black irreverence seemed to cheer Francie up and she laughed. She hadn't felt particularly well, she continued with a rueful smile, but it didn't do to bother the doctors with petty complaints. They were busy people with important things on their plate and, after all, they had a lot of sick people to deal with.

11

Anna kept softly brushing, not so much hair as wisps, seeking to arrange them in a way that would be flattering, seeking above all to soothe, to calm, to keep her mother protected from all that she could feel was coming, some gravity that her mother continued to miraculously defy. She smelt her mother. Resting her lips on her mother's scalp, she kissed her as gently as she could and inhaled her odour as greedily as possible.

Perhaps Terzo was right. Perhaps it could even go on, just like this.

12

Spring brought no revival in Francie's health. She would now often fall asleep mid-sentence, mouth agape, breath being drawn in a stuttering slow wheeze—as if by a failing pump—and she might as abruptly awake to address Anna as her mother or Terzo as her father or Tommy as her husband, and with each of them she was always the better for seeing them, whoever they were or weren't. And she would smile, revealing what remained: a defiant, joyful spirit and several yellow teeth, one gold-crowned.

Increasingly, the only time her mind seemed to offer up some form of coherence was when she looked out her window and saw the button grass plains extending, the cave and its shadows, the wind rising ruffling her clothes, the damp peaty brackish air filling her nostrils and cooling her fevered brow, and once more she would be wandering through those forbidding places with their many one-eyed strangers.

Anna tried to pretend her mother's mind was simply weary, that it was not breaking into fragments and receding. Yet the evidence was spread all over her mother's bed every time Anna visited now, incontrovertible, undeniable, damning. It lay scattered as a wild disarray of newspaper sheets—some crumpled, others balled, some upside down. Francie managed to read a few articles, but it was as if meaning came and went in a sentence, and struggle as she did, she could retain no sense of the story.

It lay there on her bed table in a child's notebook with its teddy bear cover in which she would find Francie, pen in hand, concentrating on writing down what she said were stories from her childhood. Her seeming fluidity on the page hid a different truth. Over the days and weeks the pages of the teddy bear notebook filled with a mysterious script that at first impression was neatly composed writing, but which, on closer inspection, was no more than an image of writing. Most letters appeared to be drawn side on or upside down or back to front, sometimes a mirror image of a letter, at other times the curlicue from one letter married to the foot of another, or vice versa, a script forever dissolving, melting, reforming, and in which no solid footing could be found.

Yet this image of writing, unreadable and unknowable, extending over many pages, meant something to Francie. For as long as she was writing Francie knew what the story was and where it was going. It was only after she stopped and went to read back what she had written that she would be at a loss to understand a word.

And she would laugh and laugh.

Nothing in the world struck her as funny as thinking her words meant something when she had all the time merely been playing out a long, elaborate joke at her own expense. It was hard to believe that anything could have afforded her more pleasure, not even discovering in those back-to-front and upside-down letters the lost story itself. Every letter was no more or less than a mystery that could not denote anything beyond loss, confusion, bewilderment.

Anna guessed that's how the world came to her mother by then, something so badly fractured she couldn't put any of it together in her mind. Try as she might it was impossible, but try she did, as if everything gathering around her—the nurses, the machines, the tubes, the pain, the acrid chemical taste in her mouth from the different drugs they fed her—as if all these were scattered iron filings and if she just could exert the magnet of her mind long enough, strongly enough, she could pull them into an orderly and recognisable pattern that was her life.

But of course she couldn't.

Amidst the mess of scattered paper, Anna would sometimes spot a novel Francie was reading, Philip Roth's *Sabbath's Theatre*, the book a nurse had inexplicably loaned Francie when she had asked for something modern to read, the same book she had been reading for three months, a red bookmark appearing at one time near the end of the book and at other times at the beginning or middle, and Francie erratically reading only words that were now no more sensical to her than anything else, one more failed anchor that she still fought to hold on to.

At the beginning, when her grasp on words and reality had been stronger, she had asked if people really had that sort of sex now?

When Anna, embarrassed, replied she wasn't sure, that *Sabbath's Theatre* was now in its way an old book, that these days things were again different, but yes, she suspected that, perhaps, yes, they did, Francie brightly replied, Bugger!

But her determined reading of the novel had in recent weeks become, or so it seemed to Anna, a form of almost demented courage, as if she were searching its pages ever more frantically for some map, some compass of a type that no book offers. One day while Francie was staring at that book she turned, grabbed her daughter's wrist, dragged her arm to the bed, and, looking up into her eyes, begged Anna to take her home.

Please let me live with you, she said.

13

It was too much. With her mother's physical needs it would mean Anna would have to stop work, or hire people to be in the house all day, a large and very unwelcome intrusion, full of so many difficulties and irritations. Anna resented the insinuation that it be the daughter and not either son who would be called upon for such sacrifice. More than too much, it felt wrong, and more than wrong, it was impossible.

But in her heart Anna felt it wasn't impossible. In her heart Anna felt it was hard. Very hard. But not impossible. Why could her mother not die peacefully at her daughter's home rather than live in torment in hospital? She felt it was a test, and that she had failed miserably. She realised she had not known until now that it was a test. And tested, she knew. She was not the equal of her mother, whom she had so cruelly abandoned to the loneliness and anguish of an institution. She was, she realised, a coward.

She said nothing in reply to her mother.

Like a child her mother promised to be no trouble.

And like a monster Anna told her mother no.

14

After her daughter's refusal Francie grew too weary to talk, or there was really nothing more to say, and her face turned to her window and the view beyond. She stared, lost in exhaustion, or reflection, or both, or something else altogether—betrayal, memories, prayer, regrets—it was impossible to know. After a long period of silence she turned back to her daughter.

There is so much beauty in this world, Francie said in a soft crackle, as if astonished by a discovery that had taken an entire life to be revealed. And yet we never see it until it is too late.

FOUR

1

To evade her mother's eyes Anna focused on Francie's bedspread and the hospital earphone that lay there. From it there came the distant tinny sounds of a song. It was vaguely familiar, something from her childhood. After a moment she recognised the twelve-string guitars, the horns, the harmonies, the tumbling piano refrain as 'I Go to Pieces'. Banality with a backbeat, thought Anna, the perfection of sixties pop's three-minute genius, tight as a sonnet, ridiculous as first love.

She followed the distant receding melody to where it was trapped somewhere too far away to ever know again, that same place where Ronnie was. Ronnie with whom she associated a brightness of morning light, the taste of waves, a kick of mischief that had always drawn her and others to him, a momentary buzz summoned by a handful of sixties songs, bright, brittle,

Kodachrome-coloured melodies that quickly faded like old plastic margarine tubs disintegrating in the sun at Hawley Beach where they had then lived. How much she loved him! How terribly she missed him! The boom of waves shuddering the little vertical board cottage that was their home, sand on lino, the crackling of the morning fire, Horrie's black pudding frying, those clear days when Melbourne radio made it all the way from Australia, the great world reaching across the vast ocean to their remote island, the distant tinny sound of 'I Go to Pieces' on 3AW, the sky so blue, so brilliant, so vast, so long ago that she would close her eyes and turn to the flesh-hued sun and feel the world once so big and inviting like clothes you might one day hope to grow into, and at its warm centre, as guide, as emblem, its brightest flower, Ronnie.

What happened? What happened?

2

Francie was talking to Anna about the plain of fires beyond the window when Terzo arrived. Almost immediately he was irritated and began arguing with Francie, telling her that her dreams were not to be taken seriously, that they were vile delusions brought on by her meds, and that she should stop talking about them as if they were the truth.

It wasn't enough for Terzo that their mother had

not died. It wasn't enough that she lived in her sea of waking dreams. In Terzo's view, she had to *live like us*, rationally, in a rational universe. And as there was to be no death, nor could there be any other life.

Francie looked up at Anna for support. Anna stared past her mother. She did not defend her or her visions. And Terzo kept on with his ranting, his anger seemingly without end.

3

Finally, he stopped. And when Francie turned back from staring out of her window and spoke, her watery eyes strangely, fiercely resolute, her tone was now entirely different; quiet, yet certain.

You best be on your way, was all she said. Both of you.

4

Anna returned to Sydney. Tommy asked his son, Davy, to sit with Francie to keep her company. Anna chipped in to pay him and tried not to think of it as guilt money. Life resumed its normal patterns of work and its obligatory worries—the project blowouts, the design compromises, the dilemmas of staff, the impossibility of collaborators, clients and contractors. And further crowding out thoughts of her mother's plight were the trivia of friends' lives, her own worries about her son, the minutiae of her insomnia, the tedium of cleaning and cooking and commuting, the mania of movement that seemed so much of her work.

And in that mundane world to which Anna had returned, her missing finger transformed into an enigma, a mystery she wished to unlock. She rang her doctor's surgery for an appointment to deal with a *finger issue*. When asked by the doctor's receptionist if her problem was urgent she replied that it wasn't really because, as far as she could see, it really wasn't; and so an appointment was made for ten days' time.

Three days later her left knee vanished.

5

Anna was staying at Meg's apartment in Rozelle, undressing for bed, when she noticed something odd about her left leg. When she ran her hand up and down her leg the fleshier feel of the thigh simply merged into the bonier feel of the calf. It was as if the whole were a tapered sausage, stiffened by one long bone with rubber at its pivot point, for when she went to bend it there was no pain and no problem with the leg.

She sat down and stood up. She did a squat. She did a second squat. A high kick. She attempted a star jump. Panting heavily it dawned on Anna that while these exercises might bring on a heart attack, the leg performed all its normal functions as a normal leg should.

It was just that where once a knee had done necessary knee-like things—things that inexplicably were clearly no longer necessary—there was now nothing. There was no joint connecting her thigh to her calf.

There was no knee.

Anna felt very strange. Not shocked, as she had been with the lost finger, not panicked. Just strange. Admittedly her legs had never been her best feature, though men had seemed to find them attractive enough when she was young. But what didn't men find attractive when you were young? And what did men find attractive when you were old? In recent years her legs had thickened. There was a rear view of her thighs which she had never seen and never wished to see. There was ever more hair. Her left knee, like her right, had begun to look like a rumpled bed cover. On cold days it ached. It wasn't much of a knee.

But now it had vanished she realised she missed it. But like the aurochs it was gone. Like the thylacine and the Walkman. Like long sentences. Like smoke-free summers. Gone, never to return.

6

Meg had fitted her mouthguard to stop her teeth grinding of a night, one more reason pillow talk had become an increasingly abstract concept for Anna and Meg. Meg would fall asleep, making noises halfway between a cow masticating and a growling dog on Mogadon. Not that Anna had ever heard either. But she had heard Meg. Anna called it grubbling.

She whispered Meg's name into her back. In reply, Meg let out a low bray that drifted into a sleepy sigh. Anna whispered that she thought her knee may have disappeared. Meg made more noises at an even lower frequency. At which point Anna yelled: Stop fucking grubbling! Meg! My knee has gone! *And you don't even care!*

Meg sat up and took out her mouthguard. She asked if Anna could still walk and she replied, yes, Meg, *of course*, as if it were the most stupid question in the world and it was obvious that knee or no knee she would always be able to walk.

Okay, Meg said. Meg asked if it hurt and Anna said it didn't.

Okay, Meg said. Meg asked how she could walk without a knee and Anna said she had no idea.

Okay, Meg said. She put her mouthguard back in, lay back down, grubbled something soothing and within a minute was asleep.

After a time Anna spooned into Meg. She felt the inside of Meg's knee cup the unexpected weirdness of her own kneeless leg. But what she was feeling she had no idea. She would have to ring the doctor's surgery to cancel the appointment. What would she say, she wondered as sleep enveloped her. She could say that her finger was no longer a problem that concerned her. Yes, she thought, yes, that much was true.

7

And then everything fell apart.

8

At first slowly and then quickly, at the beginning small details that only later acquired their significance, until there was an avalanche of bad news about Francie's health, a gathering wild rush downwards.

One week Tommy rang to say that Francie had been suffering incontinence. The next week Tommy called back and his voice was different.

Poor Tommy! That stammering way of speaking when he was nervous, one could say almost effeminate, such a contrast, Anna always thought, to Terzo's strong voice making its simple declarations and giving its straightforward commands. Tommy should have been a Sufi singer, Terzo would say—in that Terzo way, as though cruelty were a compliment—those rising and falling undulations heading for some transcendence that in our dear Tommy's case never quite arrives. And even Tommy would laugh as they always laughed at their brother's callousness.

Tommy continued stammering, telling how Francie had been going so well, how he had even taken her out of the hospital to visit some old relatives. And because she was going so well, and because a bad bladder was one of a dozen minor things he hadn't wanted to worry them with, they were both so busy and *h-h-* . . . anyway, he went on, the doctors had inserted a catheter, and that, in turn, had led *t-t-t*-urinary tract infection.

No, he didn't know why.

Tommy said there was no need for Anna to come home to see Francie. The doctors had said they would get on top of it, of course they would, and Francie would be fine. And when Tommy next rang to tell her that their mother, staggering to the toilet one morning without using her walking frame, had fallen and fractured her femur, Anna wasn't overly concerned. The fracture, near the top of Francie's thigh, was thankfully small and with bed rest it was expected to heal just fine.

Five days later Tommy called again at midnight. This time the stammering lasted a good half minute. And at the end Anna booked the first flight to Tasmania she could get. It left Sydney at six the following morning.

9

They met at Tommy's home, a seventies project house in Howrah, already stuffy with morning heat, all low ceilings and tiny rooms and clear-finish pine furniture and joinery. You could flee such pine alone, thought Anna.

Tommy was stammering—that he had met with the doctors. Francie's condition, far from getting better, had worsened. Terzo, who had also flown in, said he thought they were going to get on top of the urinary tract infection.

Tommy said they didn't.

And then in one clear sentence the bad news popped out.

The urinary tract infection had led to blood poisoning, which in turn had triggered a renal collapse. Francie's kidneys no longer worked.

Terzo flinched, but it was momentary. That *was* bad news, he agreed. But not the worst, he said, and his face brightened. It would be tough to go onto dialysis, he said. But how much better than dying?

And without a single slipped consonant Tommy told them that if Francie was going to be put on dialysis she'd be on it already. The hospital's policy was not to offer dialysis to anyone over eighty-five years of age.

Francie was eighty-seven.

10

For a moment even Terzo had nothing to say. When Anna managed to ask why there was such a policy, Tommy said they had told him it was on the grounds that there was no point. That was what they said. That under dialysis the quality of life of the very aged is terribly reduced while the prognosis remains bad and is often even worse. Her life could be said, Tommy went on in a quiet manner, to not really be a life at all. She would be unable to do anything; she'd either be plugged into a dialysis machine or sleeping off the effects. She could hardly be said to be living. Tommy said the doctors argued that given Francie's numerous other health problems there was the risk of many possible, potentially fatal, complications.

That's what they said.

Terzo asked how?

Tommy wasn't exactly sure how. When Terzo pressed for the doctor's name Tommy wasn't even sure who. They had names and personalities, Tommy said, of course, one was a woman and one was a man, but he had forgotten who was who, really one doctor quickly became the next, or the one before was back, there was no sense of progress or development, because no doctor was ever the last doctor and every doctor was the same doctor and all conversations never really began or ended but simply circled; they would read the notes they would babble they could never really say with conviction that Francie looked better or worse or seemed to be bouncing back or falling away. Instead they talked of vital obs, blood counts, levels, and other measurements. Yes no maybe anything.

Tommy found some notes he had scrawled on an envelope. Francie's doctors were recommending what they termed *non-aggressive renal care*. It wasn't, Tommy read aloud, withdrawal of care, or refusal to not care, but managing their mother's various issues with *an intensive approach that prioritised comfort*.

Whatever that means, said Terzo.

Y-y-y-I know, said Tommy. I am just telling you—

What they told you?

What they told me.

When Anna asked how long this would go on for Tommy drew the envelope away from his eyes to better focus and said v-v-hard to predict with any degree of precision.

They talked about exactly what these phrases might mean. Really, it was impossible to know.

If non-aggressive renal care meant their mother wasn't exposed to unnecessary awful things, said Anna, then wasn't that what they should be doing? Not insisting on the *other things*?

Even Terzo was coming around to the idea when he asked Tommy how long the doctors thought someone might live with this form of care as opposed to dialysis.

Tommy said he'd already told them. Perhaps a week, perhaps two. Maybe even more.

Terzo began yelling at Tommy that he had said no such thing, as if his brother were in on a plot to murder their mother.

85

Tommy stammered that he had.

Terzo yelled that all Tommy had said was that it was hard to predict.

Tommy stammered that no one could say if it would be next Tuesday at nine or Saturday at two; obviously doctors weren't clairvoyants.

Terzo shook his head and once more he asked, how long?

And Tommy said two or three weeks. At the most. No more.

11

Terzo went quiet, which, Anna thought, was always Terzo at his most terrifying. After a time he hissed that the doctors were feral abacuses; how it was just a cost thing for the medical system. In a clipped, almost prissy voice she always thought of as his broker's voice, the voice that told clients to man up when they'd lost six or seventy million on this or that trade, he asked why the hospital would spend money on someone who the doctors have decided will die anyway?

Tommy was beside himself; stammering and stuttering, cheeks awobble and lips aquiver, it never ceased to annoy Anna, waiting for him to form words. They had said, Tommy now spluttered, that there was no more that could be done; that *we have moved to the next phase.*

As if dying were just a phase like adolescence, and

not death itself, thought Anna. She looked at her phone she checked Instagram she read professors of health were calling for cities to be readied for mass evacuation Indigenous people fearing central Australia is becoming too hot for humans towns running out of water Australia ending its hottest year ever while someone was saying that it wasn't, that official weather records had been forged to make Australia look colder in the past and hotter now. It wasn't that these things were fragments, thought Anna. The world was fragments. She liked a meme she reposted she followed she no longer knew if the fires were already over even though they hadn't really yet begun. Things that happened yesterday were things happening today and things that hadn't happened tomorrow were old news several months ago. Was it only just yesterday was it the future now?

12

Putting her phone down Anna told Tommy that it was clearly of no matter to the doctors if Francie died. Simple as that. Terzo began yelling once more. In a way, their bullying Tommy was an old game that had begun long ago, after Ronnie died.

Tommy said he felt that it was almost as if he were being accused—only to stall mid-sentence. He recovered, he said he had to deal with this every day, he was on his own here, he had to make the best decisions he could in the circumstances.

Terzo told Tommy he wasn't on his own, that was ridiculous, no one was criticising Tommy.

But it wasn't true, thought Anna. Even if it suited them to let Tommy believe it. Tommy sobbed, saying they thought he'd failed their mother, that he was a failure.

They let Tommy believe that also.

13

But that wasn't true either. After all, Tommy had been the one there with their mother in recent years, taking her meals daily; dealing with her bills, fixing her broken window latches, door locks and faulty whitegoods, keeping her house functioning, taking her to an ever growing number of appointments and sitting with her in the waiting rooms of audiologists, optometrists, dentists, GPs and specialists; he had cooked, cleaned and washed for her, often even sleeping over in the growing confusion and mounting squalor that had overwhelmed their once fastidious mother's home on those nights Francie was fearful, or just worried.

And the memory of food squashed to black grease slicks in the carpet, the fetid toilet, the stinking bedding made Anna gasp. It was that which always broke her heart. The filth her mother finally ended up living in and never saw.

And it was Tommy who, as best he could, dealt with these things.

Not her.

Not Terzo.

Tommy.

And she found Tommy's selflessness irritating precisely because she did not have it. At such moments she felt small and mean, but she did not have it and she hated her brother who did.

She did not have it and, shameful as it was to admit, she saw Tommy's selflessness as a form of weakness and she despised him all the more for this weakness. In her heart she knew Terzo felt the same, which was why, together, they missed no opportunity to punish Tommy for his good heart. She knew why she did not know why.

She just did.

14

Terzo told Tommy he was doing a great job.

Anna told Tommy he was doing a really great job.

Tommy teared up, sobbing that he had tried, but it was so hard, so bloody hard.

Sure, Terzo said.

The more time he put in helping their mother live independently the worse things became and the more dependent Francie grew; sometimes Tommy wondered if his help simply provoked her decline.

Yes, Anna said, as though he were somehow not to blame and yet really was.

Sure, Terzo said.

Tommy sobbed some more. What could he do? he asked his siblings. He had run out of ideas.

Yes, she said, as though he were being merely irritating, yes, yes, Tommy.

She was being cruel to him and she didn't know why she was being cruel, but that was how it was between them, the confessions and the cruelty, the sympathy and the sobbing, it made her sad, even appalled, but still they continued.

He did what he could, Tommy was saying, but he could not argue with white-coated professionals. They had a way of presenting no choice as a choice, as if death were both inevitable and optional. How was that a choice? How was that a good thing? No, they had to do something. But it was beyond him.

FIVE

1

The three doctors who arrived to meet the family the next morning were polite in a professional sort of way, the sort of way that Anna always found a studied superiority. *She spoke he said they insisted* modern care informed consent they laid out odds that were no odds at all, a rigged race that could be run only one way, insisting on what Francie's fate would be. Wasn't their job to save, thought Anna, not condemn?

Francie meanwhile seemed unable to pierce the fog that daily enveloped her a little more. There was no way to inform her of what was happening. How could she consent to anything? Perhaps to preserve her dignity, to give the appearance of lucidity, she now agreed with everyone and everything, giving a slight nod every so often, even if it was irrelevant. Mostly it was. If they told her to run naked around the hospital three times she'd do it, Terzo said. Except, Tommy pointed out, Francie couldn't even sit up without help.

Anna felt for her phone she pretended something urgent had arrived. She said she was sorry she said work she stared solemnly at her screen. There was something perversely comforting in the mounting horror the sixth extinction rising oceans, the Antarctic having just had its hottest day ever while there in the air-conned ward it was cool. The forecast for Hobart was for 41 degrees, it was Tasmania for God's sake, the Switzerland of the south, *please*, no one had ever seen weather like it, it kept on and on even now it was spring or was it autumn or still winter? She thought of the fire smoke smog that lay over Sydney smearing morning into midday into afternoon with no shadow or sky to tell you otherwise, a confusion of time that was growing within her also. Was it today or yesterday or tomorrow? All these things pressed on her in an immediate way her mother did not, and in a way she did not want her mother to.

The scans show, one doctor began another went on *average count down but only on average—concurrent to strengthening a weakening that may—up pain relief to make breathing comfortable though this may mean increased discomfort of—*

Until the three children were again lost.

2

As Anna listened to the doctors talk of various new tests, medicines changing in quantity and type, the alteration of certain nursing regimes, it was as if Francie's body, now little more than skin clutching the sticks of her bones, was not that of a frail old animal but an intricate twenty-first-century machine that could be kept working with the body's technicians and engineers ceaselessly oiling, replacing, lubricating and fuelling its various mechanical parts. And somehow this approach seemed immensely crude to Anna, but why it was crude or what could be done instead she had no idea.

And when she thought about it later, she wondered if perhaps all this qualified language, this terminal lack of clarity, was both a pretence and a truth, both a howl of arrogant defiance and an admission of humility, because everyone was going to die, and Francie sooner than most, and all that could be done for any of us were the small things around the edges and not one of those small things, in the end, made any difference.

Was that all that was really possible, wondered Anna. An ever more elaborate daily changing of dirty sheets, a lengthening ritual of care and concern, as necessary and as empty as every other ritual? What if all that finally remained was just one more form of faith healing? Was it so different, thought Anna, to shamans chanting over the sick and magically plucking birds out of bellies?

Almost as a reflex, she said brightly, Sorry! It's work!

And turning away from her mother she again checked her phone. She felt numb she opened Instagram she saw newly homeless camping on beaches shanty towns appearing everywhere. Fires were burning in rainforest that never burnt it wasn't even the start of the fire season experts were saying any defence of homes will have to be abandoned as fires will now be too big and overwhelming. The water wasn't safe to drink, someone posted, no power no comms. It looked like Delhi maybe they were the new third world? She reposted a video she hadn't watched on Rem Koolhaas interiors when Terzo said the family felt dialysis was a better option, Anna looked up and nodded, murmuring assent, while the specialists' language became at once more direct and more opaque *they spoke they said* damaging dangerous they advised against not hospital policy, yes, Anna said, yes.

And yet this advice didn't feel to her like advice at all, it was delivered like a wrecking ball, with the weight of irrefutable knowledge, with the certainty of experience accumulated over years and decades, freighted with centuries of suffering witnessed and alleviated and caused, an immense weight that crushed any human feeling.

Against it their objections felt trite, even sentimental, brittle and easily broken things founded only on the weakest of emotions, pity. People, dead birds, ash. And as they continued talking the doctors' explanations once more became a thicket of words beyond the three siblings' comprehension but their meaning was clear.

3

Their mother was to die. They were to agree.

4

Over the next few days Francie declined rapidly. To hear her by then the children had to lean in very close to her lips. Everything in their mother's utterances was adrift and broken on an unseen sea, a mystery the three of them strained to divine into meaning, if they could just hear it.

The frames that held conversation—time, logic, grammar—were collapsing. Her speech was now an act of concentrated effort on the part of both speaker and listener. As it became little more than the slightest exhalations of breath shaped as best her exhausted body could with faltering throat and failing tongue, Anna and Terzo alternated between whispering platitudes to their mother by her bedside and talking incessantly on their phones in hospital corridors—extending their stay day by day, cancelling meetings, delaying decisions, absenting themselves perilously, or so it felt, from the politics of work.

Anna would say she had to check emails she would go to the bathroom she would sit on a toilet. It was hot, it was always hot, the water restrictions were already in place, the taps a trickle. She would scroll the country would burn she would watch a video shot by firefighters inside a fire truck swallowed by fire try to escape tunnelling through a phone screen of pure flame, flame moving like water giant rolling and breaking waves of fire, firefighters dead, a politician in board shorts holidaying in Hawaii, arms around people drinking tossing a shaka, *hanging loose.* There was no mention of vanishings. Two things and nothing bringing them together. Two things four, tossing a shaka meant something or it meant nothing four things, eight things twelve. A world burning and nothing bringing it back. It was possible to feel nothing it was necessary to feel nothing, the news feeds and social media feeds made you feel absolutely nothing: she could do nothing she would do nothing she was nothing. That was good. Other than keep her mother alive as everything died, nothing. She would flush the toilet she would watch the world die let her mother live *nothing nothing nothing.*

5

Francie drifted between sleep and an ever vaguer consciousness, and, in some strange symmetry, so too Anna, who when she wasn't at her mother's bedside was expecting the call from the hospital to say come back straight away, her mother was ailing, her mother was dying, her mother was dead, come back to our world now, straight away, the world of the hospital, where, once inside, there was only the inside—natural light, air, sound, noise, scent, replaced by hospital light, hospital odour, hospital noise.

It always felt half dark even when fully, overly lit, half alive although it stopped death and healed, half there and half not, Anna thought. Everything seemed to be in danger of slipping away once inside; time went too quickly, a kitchen clock racing forwards and backwards, days passing in hours, or time did not move at all, and seconds took decades to pass. Place, home, no more than a minimal landscape of paper curtains, plastic gurneys, strangers in scrubs, patient monitors, ventilators, defibrillators, ECG machines, anaesthesia machines, systems in which the interchangeable parts weren't so much the endless plastic componentry, clothing and beeping machinery but people, as if the entire system existed not to keep the patients going but, rather, the patients existed to keep the system going. And Francie, having been disconnected from the systems, was nearing the end of her usefulness to that strangest of demi-mondes.

6

On the fifth day after the doctors had told them there would be no reprieve, Francie seemed—if only momentarily—to recover some strength and purpose. And when Anna leant down to her mother's face her mother didn't turn to look at her but kept looking straight ahead, as if to save all her strength for the single message she then delivered in a hoarse whisper.

I want. The rites read. Annie.

Her words croaks punctuated by painful swallows.

Best. Call for the. Priest.

Anna looked at her phone for news.

7

Her brothers were standing at the end of the bed. She whispered to them. She went to the bathroom she sat on a toilet she ignored her non-knee she looked at her phone she looked at photos. Incinerated kangaroos in foetal clutches of fencing wire charred koalas burnt bloated cattle on their backs, legs in the air, growing out of dry river beds. She scrolled past medieval tableaux of muted humanity on beaches in the ochre wash of an inferno. Caravaggio Brueghel Bosch it seems to have happened a very long time ago it's happening today is it the terracotta that lights everything now? You ask people when the fire hit, someone says somewhere, but they can't remember they don't know what day it is. Days months years blur. Light blurs words slide her phone beeped with a message. Anna couldn't bear to read it she couldn't bear to think. Shoes dresses kitchenware. She couldn't stand Instagram she opened Insta. A generator with an electric light illuminating a fire-created darkness at midday when did the world turn black? Hell in a wildfire nothing in the palm of the hand. There was something there was everything.

There was nothing.

When Anna came back to the ward her brothers were waiting in the corridor. Terzo whispered something about the priest. She looked at the way his shoulders bunched when he was angry, and turned her ear not so much to hear her brother as to avoid him. More loudly he told her that to have a priest meant only one thing. Having taken the final sacrament and accepted her death as imminent, Francie would lose the desire to go on any further and will herself to death. Anna's phone wouldn't properly load her Facebook feed, it was a relief it was agony it was clear this would sabotage (Terzo's words) their attempts to keep Francie alive even though the doctors had made it clear that keeping her alive was an impossible task. It was maddening for Terzo. The doctors *and* now their mother.

She doesn't want to die, Terzo said adamantly as they stood in the hospital corridor, emphasising the point with a skinny white finger, as though that proved things. And, he added, we don't want her to die.

Her Facebook still wouldn't load. Was it the hospital walls?

No, Anna said, shaking her head.

No, Terzo said, you're right.

Tommy said that was all well and fine, but think of the pain, the torment, that could result from keeping her alive. He wasn't sure he could be that cruel. Why should anyone suffer so much for so long?

Terzo began speaking over him, saying how the only thing was to live. To live! he hissed. To live!

The only mistake was to fear mistakes, he went on, the only death to accept death. Saying Francie had had a good run (though no one had said that) was such a stupid thing, a self-fulfilling, lazy, even a criminal thing.

Death upset Terzo, thought Anna, not only the fact of it but the very idea of it. Every life, he used to say in his Hallmark moments, was an affirmation of the universe. And perhaps that was why, Anna sometimes thought, every death was a terrifying question that Terzo had been unable to answer since Ronnie died.

And yet something about that terrible will of Terzo would paralyse both Anna and Tommy. Tommy would always end up seeking to appease Terzo and she would always submit. The effect was the same: Terzo would get his way.

But bending their mother to his will was not so easy. That day, at first anyway, even Terzo had no answer to their mother's wishes.

As he continued to rage Anna went back to the bathroom. A news feed loaded, maybe it wasn't the hospital walls maybe it was her phone maybe she needed a new one. Dense fire smoke ultra-fine PM2.5 particles, small enough to damage lungs and bloodstream smothering Sydney, anything over 200 hazardous, levels at 2200.

She googled vanishings. Nothing. She posted a penguin meme she couldn't hold her thoughts she couldn't read she clicked through smoke sending people crazy it triggers anxiety a professor said it's like a war the enemy is attacking the city we don't know where the enemy is. The planet's life support systems may collapse flat earth believers now number millions new words for a new age, reads a meme. *Pyro-cumulonimbus* giant fire-generated clouds sixteen kilometres high creating more fire through lightning, ember attacks, wind, fire tornadoes. *Omnicide. Solastalgia* emotion induced by the loss of everything. What is the image for nothing? Where is a language she thought she didn't she tried Insta again it loaded. So much joy! Instagram, blessed Novocaine of the soul! Foodholidayssmilinggroupsshopping. She had to get off. She knew it. She had to get off.

8

Though Francie had asked for the priest, though she wanted the last rites, the absolution, the public recognition that her time on earth was now ending, she did not seem God-obsessed as her mother—known to all simply as the Tiger—had been. Dying twenty-two years earlier, clutching her rosary beads as if they were a lifeline, the Tiger had muttered her Hail Marys with a barely contained terror that her children also understood as a bitterness and the wild, fearful begging for forgiveness of a young girl got pregnant out of wedlock. Try as she might to atone, the Tiger understood her God as one more hard old man who would not forgive her that terrible sin, the wages of which would be eternal punishment in the flames of hell. What frightened her was not death but what came after. She knew it; she knew it, she would say, and no matter how many decades of the rosary were chanted she was one more of the doomed. She had outlived her thirteen brothers and sisters as well as her husband, outlived even some of her own children, but she could not outlive her cruel God's implacable judgement of a woman conceiving out of wedlock. This waking idea of death waged war with another dreaming idea that came to her in her sleep in those last weeks of her life.

The old people, as she called them—all the dead: family, friends, some so remote she only recognised them from details in half-remembered stories—came to her each night on a dray and asked her to go with them; across a sun-drenched field of freshly cut hay they came, Come with us! they would call every evening, Come with us, Kitty!

And every night the Tiger refused, fearing a trap made by God, a trap she had eluded for so long, so successfully, warding it off with pious acts and a ferocity of life force. But even she had to die in the end, at ninety-nine, swearing until almost her last breath that she was a year younger, a confusion to help explain the baby born two months after her marriage, the one she beat with all the ferocity and horror that only the truly damned can show for their greatest sin, the daughter they christened Frances.

9

And as the Tiger had wanted to live because she was ashamed of her sin, thought Anna, perhaps Francie was perfectly content to die because she wasn't ashamed of her own life. But Terzo was determined to save their mother from her own wishes. As it was clear that she now very much wished to die he insisted that they must do everything to keep her alive.

Tommy, in an uncharacteristically assertive manner, asked that as she wished to die shouldn't they let her? Wasn't that her wish?

Who in Francie's position wouldn't wish to die? Terzo replied. That wasn't the point—the point was that they had to *change* Francie's position. Only then would her wishes also change. They would not call for the priest.

And when Tommy objected again Terzo, looking frustrated, added the caveat, of course we will call for the priest when she's ready. *But just not yet.*

Anna wondered if calling for the priest was about God at all. Maybe it was about them. Maybe it was a way of Francie saying to her children: enough. *Please.* Let me go.

But they could not allow that.

They would decide. Not her. Not God. And her time was not to be now.

It felt very cruel, Anna thought. And perhaps that's because it was.

They went back into the ward, where Terzo gently told their mother that they would call for the priest when she was going to die. *But*, he added, smiling that terrifying corporate grin, all teeth and treachery, she was going to live.

10

That night Anna met Terzo for a counter meal at Tom McHugo's. Something came up about counselling. Terzo said he once underwent some sessions after his second marriage ended. He would tell the counsellor about aspects of his life, explain what he made of them, and then the counsellor would agree with him, congratulating Terzo on his self-awareness. The counsellor told Terzo he was one of the lucky people, one of those rare people who know who they are, and Terzo agreed with the counsellor.

After a few weeks the game changed a little, with the counsellor repackaging Terzo's words as her words, offering Terzo back to Terzo. Perhaps, he supposed, it was to justify her very large fee. In any case, Terzo kept going and they kept agreeing and then Terzo stopped going.

If he was honest, he told Anna, he rather missed it. He didn't mind talking about himself, but he felt he more or less had the measure of his own sorrows. They were knowable and thus containable and therefore controllable. But finally he had enough of them being invoiceable and he stopped the consultations.

She asked if he had talked about Ronnie's death. If he had—

Terzo's wine glass shattered on the floor.

Sorrysorrysorry! he mumbled, sounding oddly like Tommy. He kept looking down at the floor, making no movement. Anna went to the bar and returned with a dustpan and broom to find his head still bowed. She was too embarrassed to step into his gaze and clean up the mess.

For a long time he stared at the broken glass on the floor. They were in a corner of the bar below a speaker, and she realised that the music was masking wet choking noises her brother was making.

She softly called his name. His gaze remained fixed on the floor. It was as if he had to empty something out of himself and yet the more he emptied it out the larger it grew within. He shook his head. Finally, without looking up he asked if she remembered the Tiger's dream of the dray and the old people coming to fetch her?

Anna nodded.

And Ronnie?

Anna said nothing. Of course she knew the dream: as she was dying the Tiger had told the family repeatedly how the old people who came to take her away every night were led by a fine looking young man who stood on the dray, reins in hand. And that handsome man was Ronnie, all grown up. At the time, Ronnie was fourteen. It was a strange detail, given all the others who came each night in her dreams were the long dead.

He didn't say that ten days after they buried the Tiger, Ronnie, home on holiday from his boarding school, Marist College, had hanged himself. He didn't need to say it.

Anna replied that it was coincidence, nothing more, as everyone said then and said now, and which no one really believed. Sometimes when she thought about it, Anna had a sense—ridiculous, she knew—of two worlds briefly coming too close, the living and the dead, and things becoming muddled.

He himself had been twenty-two months younger than Ronnie, Terzo said in a low voice. After that he became the child they couldn't lose. Perhaps he became many things he was never meant to be, things that he was not. You know, Terzo said, when you think about it you can make yourself anything. But you never really become it. There's always that same person hiding inside.

He had anointed himself Terzo.

Third.

The third brother.

Though he was now the second he was now nothing pretending he was still the third, that Ronnie wasn't in the shed.

11

She stepped forward and began sweeping up the glass as he kept talking, making no movement to help.

No, he said, he didn't know what the matter was with himself. For a time he thought it was sadness or grief. But it wasn't. It seemed something larger, something he couldn't explain or understand and he just kept falling through it. Did she know that feeling? That feeling of a void through which you keep falling. You know? Forever.

He was falling and falling and when he looked around he saw her, Tommy, Ronnie, Francie, he said. But he couldn't grab on to their outstretched arms, there was the gum tree they climbed as children outside the church and he was falling through it he couldn't grab the branches, he could see the way the bark curled up and peeled away, the green hope of the new bark, he could smell the ants and the Tasmanian air, but he couldn't grab hold, he kept falling through that blinding light, he kept losing his footing, falling and falling again into the darkness, and he couldn't stop falling. That was all it was. A void. Did she know that feeling? That was where he lived now.

Something seemed to wrench him and he was unable to stop himself now almost convulsing. He tried to stifle his sobs with strange animal choking sounds, dreadful, pathetic sounds, thought Anna. Much as she resented Terzo's seemingly impervious cool it was awful to see him without it, as though so much front were an exoskeleton and without it he was reduced to this.

Finally, he looked at her and said that he thought love was vanishing all around him, it was terrifying, that you could feel love vanishing everywhere, did that make sense? Did she not feel that? Terzo asked. That it was the absence of love? How could people do what they did unless love had vanished?

She said her fear was that people sometimes did what they did because of love.

He wasn't sure, and then he said that if Francie went, there would be no love left at all for him to hold on to.

His strange animal sobbing began again, almost as if he was about to throw up. But there was nothing.

It was the only time Anna ever heard him mention Ronnie's death. Terzo had found Ronnie's body hanging in the shed. He never spoke about that. She had never asked him about what he saw. It was as if he needed to vomit something but there was nothing there was something everything nothing.

Look at a cloud or painting, Terzo said after a long pause, but he couldn't continue, he went quiet again, as if the words he needed were broken and scattered over the floor amongst the shards of glass Anna had missed. In truth, he began again, and stopped. *Truth*, he said with a small laugh. He had realised he didn't know himself, that he hadn't begun to know himself, his terror was that he was so much more than the investor, the venture capitalist, the successful businessman. Not that he was an exceptional person; no, he knew there was nothing special about him. But he felt that there was within him exceptional things, that everyone had these exceptional things, but some people like him suppressed them, killed them, and that was his secret fear, that he'd killed who he really was, that he killed them after Ronnie. He didn't know why. He killed them so they wouldn't kill him. He didn't know. No. He wasn't lucky he didn't know who he was he didn't know does anybody know?

These thoughts frightened him, the idea that he was—in some fundamental sense, he couldn't understand it but he felt it—already dead inside. This idea haunted him. These thoughts had begun coming to him after Francie first fell ill, Terzo told Anna, and one night he rang Tommy for some solace, some kind words, even his brother's stammering felt as if it might help, but when Tommy answered Terzo heard only his own voice berating Tommy for not having done more to help Francie. Could she believe it? And the weird thing was that the angrier he got the calmer he felt. He felt better. That was the worst. It let him forget. It was sick, beating up on Tommy like that so he might feel better. But it let him forget.

Terzo looked at Anna, a look about which she wasn't sure. He held up a hand of his skeletal fingers in that manner he had as if halting traffic, and his voice abruptly resumed its normal commanding, slightly high-pitched certainty. He told her that she had the contact who could help their mother, she knew who he meant, he had forgotten the name, but she must remember. Without some intervention their mother had only days left. Surely Anna could do something?

And that's where it was left that evening, knowing Francie's life was now measured in weeks or perhaps days.

Unless, that is, she did as Terzo demanded.

After leaving the pub she went to the hospital. The ward lights were dimmed and in the late-night languor particular to hospitals she saw a stranger sitting silently with Francie, a man so young his thick beard seemed a bad theatre prop.

He slowly turned to her, smiled, and said, Hello, Auntie Annie.

SIX

1

After a moment's hesitation she recognised the kohl-lined dead eyes as those of Davy, Tommy's schizophrenic son. They hugged, and with their arms around each other turned back to face Francie.

In the uncertain hospital night light her mother's translucent skin appeared marbled with watery blue veins. A weak ammoniacal smell came off her as if she had been just washed in Windex. Her head rested deep within a pillow that seemed too large, like some fragile and minuscule piece of porcelain almost lost in its mounting cushion. Anna, startled by the ever-growing vermicelli of tubes running in and out of Francie, momentarily saw her mother as no longer her mother, that emaciated body now no more than a carapace of something long ago caught and killed in a spider's web.

A long moan passed out of Francie, slow wind escaping a deep chasm, and she abruptly woke, startled, and started scratching at a leg. Tommy! Tommy! she cried out. And when Davy soothed her, she turned to him and stared for some time as if she had lost something.

At other times that night she begged to be taken home, to be brought back to the hospital, fell in and out of sleep, rubbed her joints as if suffering some terrible pain, until, suddenly worried that the CIA spies were watching, she halted, suspicious. When Anna told her no one was there, Francie pointed at the window. There! There! she cried, shaking her head at her daughter's evident stupidity. *There*—those people with only one eye!

Davy was easier than his aunt with Francie's ravings. He glanced out the window, turned back around and said he didn't understand how they got away with playing cards all the time. If their supervisor caught them they'd be for the jump.

Francie seemed to calm at his observations, nodded agreement, and was a few moments later once more fast asleep.

Anna told Davy how sweet he was with Francie. Davy told her with a smile that he was used to people humouring him in his delusions. The problem, he said, was that the delusions were real.

Where did Francie go in her dreams, Anna wondered
as she watched over her that night. Was she returning
to her childhood stories of a fabulous past of rebel
priests, magic, a world where the convicts cursed and
fate answered, where sea eagles stole babies and brought
them up in nests in Bass Strait islands, where priests
froze adulterers to the spot by staring at them?

Brought up in poverty on a Depression era scrab-
bling fifty-acre farm, Francie viewed her childhood
on that north western Tasmanian hill as rich beyond
compare. Her father, whom she loved deeply, would
each morning walk down the three back steps of their
weatherboard farmhouse with its newspaper lined walls,
and drop to his knees.

And there in the Melrose hills, halfway between the
immensity of Bass Strait's ocean twenty miles to the
north and the massif of Mount Roland an equivalent
distance to the south, that tiny prostrated form let
his soul fill with the glittering azure of the sea, the
ultramarine of the mountain, and the bands between
of ploughed volcanic earth and vibrant forest and crops
rippling in the racing cloud shadow. The red! The
green! The blue! If he were to make a flag, that would
be his tricolour, and he would call it home, family, love.
If he were to shout it to the heavens he would cry Us!
We! Ours!

But he knelt.

And, kneeling there, head bowed, with the immense universe vibrating in and out and through him, that universe which he understood as him also, Francie's father would each morning thank God for such beauty that there is in this world.

The idea and the image—they were to Francie one. The insignificance and the immensity. The gift and the gratitude. The power of the man in the world, the power of the world in the man.

Francie never forgot that vision, nor did she ever escape the sense that the world and God and beauty and love could also be hers, if she just fell to her knees and let each fill her. And against the cosmic power of that image the poverty of her childhood was as nothing.

3

For all that, she was taught from the beginning not to annoy God with her prayers. The authorities in life were all men and only men, and God, really, was but one more. He's a *busy man*, Francie was told as a child by the Tiger, and in her turn Francie would say to her children, He has more important things to be bothered with than your worries. The best thing, she would advise, is to ask the Virgin Mary for help; She would help if asked, She always did; She always would; *She's one of us*.

And it was this cult of women that prevailed in their home; of the Madonna, of the Tiger, of numerous aunts and great aunts who frequently visited with strange stories of the family that vaulted the great sea wall of the First World War, of Francie herself. And to that cult they all, including Horrie, paid obeisance.

Men are better at digging ditches, Horrie would say. But that's about it.

Anna never heard her father say an ill word of the Tiger, who lived with them for thirty years, only ever speaking of her with a deep respect. Women and more women, that was more or less their home. Outwardly they knelt to God, Jesus and men, but in their hearts the order was otherwise, reversed; in their hearts it was women who were worshipped, and Horrie, even in his growing desperation to control his collapsing mind, knelt to them.

For all that, Francie had grown up in a time and place that allowed a woman little. What was permitted her? This much: them—Anna, Tommy, Ronnie, Terzo. To influence, to shape, to create. That Francie chose not to bully or dominate or control her children was, Anna only now could see, to her mother's enormous credit. Offered a petty domestic tyranny in compensation for freedom lost, Francie refused it. And not just once, but every day and every moment when a brutal response would have been so easily justified and perhaps even justifiable.

On one visit to the hospital Anna found Francie uncharacteristically sad.

I used to hit you, Francie said, and she was sobbing. I used to hit you, my poor little pets, all of you.

It was true. And it was meaningless.

Her love was large and all-encompassing, so large that her other aspects seemed trivial next to it. Even her often unexpected acts of violence towards them, what she termed *a good swipe or whack*—assorted acts of swift, brutal punishment ranging from slapping, spanking, hitting with wooden jam spoons with heads the size of small fists, to the flat of kitchen knives brought down quick and hard across the backs of unruly hands, to once chasing Ronnie around the lounge room with an iron fire poker with which she was trying to smash him in the head, crying out as she chased him, I'll give you a whack, my boy!—none of it meant anything much against her immense love.

I am sorry, Francie was saying, I am so, so sorry. I could never have hurt any of you, she said.

And Anna told their mother that she never had. Which was, in its way, true. Her mother's remorse was inexplicable to her daughter. For she had never doubted the ferocity of her mother's love.

4

Sometimes it occurred to Anna how little mention her mother made of Horrie. Francie did sometimes refer to outbursts by politicians she thought inexplicable as *burning the autumn leaves,* a reference to when she had found Horrie standing on their bed emptying pillows of their feathers onto a fire he had lit in the middle of the mattress in order to burn, he said, the autumn leaves. He was fifty-two, and his dementia could be ignored no longer. For several preceding years Francie had stoically borne his increasing lapses of memory, his growing erratic behaviour, his uncharacteristic outbursts of anger, covering them up as best she could. But after the fire she had no choice. Horrie went to a home, where he died of Alzheimer's three and a half years later.

She never really knew just how much her mother bore during those years, thought Anna. She had adored her father and she wanted her mother to adore him even more. But it wasn't Francie's style. And her mother's silence on the matter offended Anna's idea of her parents' love or of what love itself should be.

Sometimes Anna tried to draw it out by saying something sweet about her father, but this would only lead Francie to make some observation of his *ways* as she called them. Hers were wry asides, amused takes on his more exasperating habits, but there was no criticism in them. It was as if he were simply an amiable enough stranger she had happened to end up incarcerated with for life. Their relationship, in these tellings, felt entirely accidental.

Francie had married at the age of nineteen, too young too quickly, she would say. Their parents' quarrels were mostly off-stage, but Tommy once mentioned how

Francie had told him that Horrie, as his mind began to slip away, decided the house needed to be organised differently. He wouldn't allow Francie even to stack the cupboards her way and insisted that he do it instead, only to then find it impossible to recall where he put anything. In this way sardines ended up in sock drawers and socks in the shed.

Once in those final years, Tommy told Anna, Francie had broken down and cried about how their father had treated her, trying to control every aspect of her life. But he also adored her, and even if their love was stifling as well as sustaining they were still, in the end, a love story.

5

Francie delighted in tools and engines, and revered anyone with a manual skill. She would lovingly describe how beautifully her father scythed hay. She viewed her car mechanic with an awe others might reserve for a violin virtuoso. She still thrilled with wonder when recalling the steam threshing machine coming to *the district*, as she called it, a giant iron monster rumbling up the dirt tracks, belching sparks and a fiery red smoke into the night sky.

When life grew grey she cleaned her car with a thoroughness and vigour that somehow made her happy, always ending with her putting the bonnet up and rueing that she couldn't service and tune the motor. She had a fine head for mathematics and particularly loved helping them all with calculus, something for which Horrie, a council worker, had no ability.

She had trained and worked as a primary school teacher but, as was the rule in those days, she had to resign when she first fell pregnant and thereafter devoted her life to her husband and her children. Outside the house she grew to lack confidence; she played the wife and mother out of duty and finally habit, and as it was a habit that fundamentally bored her she was always glad to return home and be done with the public trappings of wifely duty, even if it only meant returning to the privations of wifely labour, living in a world where little things loomed large: the sick child she stayed up with through the night; the saucepan with the dangerous loose handle Horrie never got around to fixing; new school shoes suddenly too small; the stain in the birthday dress that she managed to remove. No one sang of it, no one celebrated it, no one respected it. Francie did all of it, agreed with none of it, and preferred simply to get on with it. But once, Anna overheard her and the Tiger speaking about women, voices strangely low and gravelly, a muted music of rage she never forgot.

6

After Horrie's death Francie returned to work as a primary school teacher. Something happened, or something didn't happen, or several things happened; in any case, she became friendly with a teacher, though whether it was sexual or not no one seemed to know. Tommy felt there was something in it but had no evidence; having no evidence, Anna felt there was nothing in it. The following year the teacher didn't return to school. Later they learnt that he had run off with a teacher's aide known only as Miss Dalcoe. Francie lost weight, and stopped dressing for effect, preferring a sombre functionality in her clothing. At the end of that terrible year she retired and never worked again.

It wasn't Francie's way to view her life with pity or regrets. If the opportunities she was afforded were few and small, her predominant take on her own life was a determined gratitude tinged with an occasional acidity in her judgements on others.

Her most damning judgements she reserved for herself. Oh, she was too stupid to do that, she might say, or, Why ask me? What would I know about anything?

And in these small put downs of her own life it was possible to sense an aching regret so vast it was not possible to imagine it could be lived with and survived.

7

On finally making it back to Sydney the following evening Anna did what she wouldn't normally do, and rang an old friend—well, not exactly an old friend, but an old boyfriend of a close friend—who now headed up the renal unit at one of Sydney's best hospitals. On the evidence she presented, the nephrologist said he had to agree that the Hobart renal team's arguments seemed sound and, besides, if it was the hospital's policy then that was most likely that.

But when in passing he mentioned a new study showing that renal care in the very elderly was sometimes a worthwhile exercise, Anna leapt on it. She deployed the charm she used on wayward clients, a solicitous and even deferential tone that cloaked something a little fierce. Perhaps more than a little fierce. She cajoled him as if he were a recalcitrant contractor who refused to understand her vision of a new building as their desire.

The eminent nephrologist conceded that she may have some valid points. Or perhaps he just took pity, or perhaps he had a memory of the attractive young friend of a long-ago girlfriend, a person who no longer existed. In any case, he finally relented, saying he knew the head nephrologist in Hobart and would put in a word.

He was at once so sweet and so authoritative, thought Anna, and she remembered how kind he had been to her friend who, to be honest, had not treated him at all kindly.

So moved by his good nature was Anna that she was

about to ask him about her missing finger and vanished knee when she heard another voice speaking and him muttering in exasperation, *Fucking nurses!*

And these words were uttered with such dismissal, in a tone she would have hated to hear turned on her if she had told him her improbable story. *Bloody Anna!* he might have cried.

No, she thought, far better she said nothing.

In any case, in this way, of a great grid of influential connections reaching out to other influential connections, a text was sent, a return call was made, and a word was put in.

8

At a dinner some weeks later at Tommy's—a Tommy-like meal he called lamb curry and which Terzo, in high spirits, christened rogan gosh—Terzo pressed his vision for their mother's future on his siblings.

For everything was changed.

Francie had been put on dialysis. If not overly positive nor were the reports negative, and there had been no further setbacks. When not on dialysis or sleeping she would sometimes talk and seemed, so Tommy told them, much less confused.

Terzo's determined approach—which was now also their approach—appeared vindicated. Their money, power and influence had proven irresistible: lobbying, pressuring, the buying in of whatever help the hospital did not provide or which it provided, in Terzo's view, inadequately or incompetently. Terzo, who had flown to Hobart from Kuala Lumpar, was triumphant, his thinking and methods now a proven success. Francie's recovery—coupled to what Terzo, in his words, described as closing a big deal with a timber logging company in Malaysia—had left him reinvigorated, almost manic, or so it seemed to Anna. When she asked him if he was worried about the large sums this was costing he leant back and answered with a joke of which he was fond: the money's neither here nor there, he said. It's in Switzerland.

Terzo talked of how the world was righting itself, and with effort, with resources, Francie's health could also be put right and she would return to her life. It was as if all these things too were neither here nor there, but also existed in a Swiss bank vault.

Revived with Francie was his determination that she could once more live in her own home. What seemed impossible only a short time ago, was now, Terzo argued, actually possible if they just put in place a web of support around her so comprehensive that it would on the one hand allow her to live for as long as was technically possible while on the other hand free her children from the burdens of drudgery and duty that looking after her might otherwise necessitate for them.

Terzo opened his phone. From some notes he began outlining what he felt was necessary in order that their mother could return to living independently and, above all, to simply living; care that they needed to buy in, specifically: live-in nurse, or several nurses if it came to that, housekeeper, reliable driver to take their mother to her numerous appointments, and on it went, so many people and things that only money and people with money could afford. Anna watched his long skinny finger scrolling, now summoning up so many other things large and small that needed attending to—physiotherapists, speech therapists, cook, gardener: more things that needed more money to buy in.

Terzo was in such a good mood, thought Anna, that not even Tommy, or Tommy's cooking, could annoy him. And still he kept scrolling down, as if his finger were a cat's paw playing with a doomed songbird. There was, he said, the matter of setting up the family home for someone in Francie's admittedly frail state—ramps, rails, handles, friendly plumbing, a new shower bay, assorted minor fix-ups and maintenance. A builder was needed.

Stroking his neatly trimmed silver stubble beneath which lay, knew Anna, his doughy chin, Terzo said it was about love.

Anna found herself oddly reassured by the certainty of Terzo's new plan. Facing their mother's decaying body which they could not let decay, Terzo's plan quickly became her plan and then her passion, and, finally, she could see, simply common sense.

9

Tommy brought out more food and as he sat back down he began stammering something about the need to accept death. While he spoke, Anna looked up at the kitchen walls where his unsold paintings hung—vivid pictures done with a wild eye and acrylic paint sculpturally applied depicting Hobart and its mountain and river, local fish, plants, and road kill. They were deeply unfashionable, and thus, to Anna, deeply embarrassing. Terzo was more charitable, perhaps because art meant so little to him. What's art but a stutter anyway, Terzo had once said mockingly to her. Hardly the main game, is it? Everybody double guessing what the last word was or what the next word might be?

Before Tommy had finished Terzo was talking over him, dismissing Tommy's point as a lazy cliché that too easily becomes a death sentence.

And it was true, for Tommy's idea of accepting death felt weak and spineless next to Terzo's mad, cruel and hateful love which Anna suddenly understood, sitting there in Tommy's wretched suburban family room, had also become her mad, cruel and hateful love. For Terzo it was simple—and she understood now why that was. To every problem of their mother's weakening flesh was their infinitely stronger cruelty. Once you accepted its necessity, it was unstoppable and impossible to defeat. She felt almost giddy with the sheer power of their cruelty. Buy in the help they needed using Francie's money—and to what better use could it be put?

Tommy stammered some more, but it really didn't mean that much to them; after all, it was just Tommy. Even when boarding with his younger brothers at Marist College he had turned to Ronnie, he, Tommy the weak one, and Ronnie the strong, the protector.

At Ronnie's funeral, while Father Michael from their school conducted the service, Tommy had stood outside the church, refusing to go inside. And after that, as Terzo used to say, *T-t-tommy* began.

Secure in their overwhelming compassion for their mother, Terzo turned to Tommy, who had acquired power of attorney over her affairs just before she had been hospitalised, and asked him to give them the rundown on their mother's finances. As Terzo put it, with a smile, they were a board of directors examining a newly acquired corporate takeover. This was the last part of the puzzle, a proper understanding of what money Francie had, the final step in their taking control of Francie's life.

And exactly *what*, Terzo asked, has the board acquired, Tommy?

But Terzo's manic energy seemed to evaporate when Tommy began telling them. He quietly said, Yes. And then over and over again, as if it were normal and not normal, like Anna's finger. *Yes yes.* They listened but what was it that they were hearing? *Yesyesyesyes.*

And as Tommy continued with his byzantine tale of papers hidden in the back of a wardrobe, of retired accountants and evasive bank officers, his stammering grew almost uncontrollable.

10

Anna inadvertently glanced at her offending hand and, realising she might be drawing attention to what she wanted no one to see, quickly looked back at Tommy, while running her hand over her knee that also wasn't. But nobody noticed, nothing changed, all that was lost remained unfound, and when she looked back down her leg still bent in the middle as if made of some new-age bendable polymer uninterrupted by the knob of a kneecap.

She had finally seen a doctor the week before in Sydney, telling her about the strange pains she'd been having in her feet, the ostensible reason for her visit. To hide her kneelessness on her way to the doctor's surgery she had worn a long skirt. But then, lying on a gurney, she had hitched up her skirt to reveal her kneeless leg. Along with her three-fingered left hand, splayed prominently on the gurney's crisp sheet, she felt that both were so obviously presented it wouldn't be necessary to tell the doctor about her real problem because it would be impossible for the doctor not to see it.

As she lay there her gaze drifted to a large framed photo on the wall depicting a gaudily clad snowboarder. Noticing this, the doctor—a tiny woman with big glasses that seemed to emphasise the child-like nature of her small face—said that the photo was of her competing *at the Pan-Pacs*. The photo showed the doctor—unrecognisably clad—crouching, suspended in the austere azure of an alpine sky as if levitating above the snow slopes. Anna ventured the observation that it wouldn't be *kind on the knees*, to which the diminutive doctor replied, Not exactly.

Anna suggested to the doctor that knees were the most *necessary* joint.

The young doctor tapped on her keyboard.

And not just for alpine sports.

The young doctor came over to the gurney.

When you thought about it, Anna continued, to lose a knee is a very tragic thing.

The doctor began massaging feet, swivelling toes, manipulating legs, prodding, tracing, touching, and with every second or third gesture asking a question, dark eyes doe-like behind her big black glasses.

Anna followed her monosyllabic answers with extended questions about the necessity of knees in all pursuits and not just snowboarding. The long-term effect of walking on knees. Of ageing on the patella.

Without answering, the young doctor went on with her investigation, leaning over to look more closely. When her long blonde hair fell over her face she flicked it back behind her neck. It was then Anna saw on that child-like head that where a child-like ear should have been there was instead the same soft blur of flesh and detail that marked the site of Anna's vanished finger and now vanished knee.

Don't be frightened, the doctor smiled, but Anna couldn't help but stare in horror at the side of the doctor's head. There was no scarring from trauma, nor distorted shapings consequent on birth deformities. Instead there was an all too familiar photoshopped sheen, the same smearing in which the world hid itself on Instagram and Facebook and a hundred other platforms and a million apps, edges of bodies without definition, carapaces warped free of bone or muscle beneath, a Kardashian Instagram error, something akin to a digital animation and no longer quite human flesh.

As the doctor continued scrutinising Anna's body she gave no indication of her intense professional focus having revealed to her Anna's missing knee or missing finger or, for that matter, having ever noticed her own missing ear. She told Anna they would need to do some blood tests to ascertain exactly what was wrong. There was a range of things a blood test could reveal, the doctor said.

Missing things? Anna suggested hopefully, seeking perhaps to steer the doctor to a certain condition.

Not exactly, the doctor said, the test only tells us what there is—an excess of mast cells, say, or a surfeit of bad fats.

The latter sounded to Anna a not unreasonable definition of her middle-aged body, even, in its way, a poetic description. And as Anna sat there pondering herself as a surfeit of bad fats sans finger and knee, the earless doctor talked on, oblivious to her own vanished ear, to her patient's vanishing body. *She spoke she spoke she said* sensible footwear reputable podiatrists, she filled out a form she handed it over, instructing Anna to take it to pathology for further blood tests.

On leaving the doctor's room Anna screwed up the form, threw it in a bin in reception and, adjusting her skirt, went home.

11

A fleck of white rice between Tommy's yellowing teeth was visible through his vibrating lips. As Anna continued staring Tommy's stammering stopped. He needed to tell them something, he said.

He stood up, went to the kitchen, filled a glass with four fingers of whisky, held the bottle up by way of question and when Terzo and Anna both shook their heads, he returned to the table.

He sat down, took a sip of his whisky and continued. It had taken him until now, Tommy said, to get a clear picture of what had befallen Francie. Not only was there not enough money in their mother's accounts, but financially speaking things were in a very bad way.

Terzo said something about thanking God for their father's super fund.

Tommy was holding the glass in front of him with both hands, staring at it as if he were lost at sea and it was a compass.

That was the beginning of the whole mess, Tommy said finally, and drained the rest of the whisky. He wiped his lips with a finger and coughed. Nine years ago, he said, Francie went to see the bank to get her affairs in order. A financial advisor persuaded her to withdraw all the superannuation and invest it in some new bank products, delivering three times the returns she had previously got. Six months later everything was gone. Everything!

To pay the bills, Tommy went on, Francie had begun borrowing from the bank using her home as security, reverse mortgaging on locked-in high interest rates. And in this way Francie had gone from being debt free with substantial savings to being highly in debt. Worse, she was very close to the tipping point where, if she lived for only another twelve months, Tommy had calculated that the remaining equity would not be enough to pay for the ongoing interest payments.

Having looked at it all thoroughly, Tommy said, unless something was done urgently their mother would soon be homeless. The only way out of the mess that he could see was to sell the family home, pay off the debt, and use what little equity remained to put a deposit on a small unit, which would be more practical in any case. He held up an envelope across which figures were scrawled. It's all here, he said. I can show you later if you want, but if anything I've probably been cheap.

He itemised annual costs of repayments on a new, smaller mortgage, rates, insurances, utilities, living costs, and multiplied them by three years to arrive at the grand total of $200,000. He had no idea what the costs for Terzo's extensive plans for their mother's ongoing care might be but it would have to be at least $30,000 a year. Multiply by three, add it to the $200,000 and they would need close to $300,000—or more.

And that, Tommy concluded, was just three years.

12

Terzo sighed—an unusual sound of resignation for Terzo—and once done sighing said he would contribute $200,000, saying he took the view that it was only money, a view, thought Anna, that it was perhaps easier for a venture capitalist to hold than Tommy, a failed artist-cum-part-time crayfisherman deckie.

Terzo knew as well as her, thought Anna, that Tommy

had nothing. She felt she had no choice but to offer up the other $100,000. Not that she had it either. She was still paying off her new apartment in Potts Point, that debt being only one of several: the outstanding payment she owed on buying into her firm's partnership, her Tesla payments, and a second mortgage on a small beach house at Byron Bay.

But she had credit. She had no money, she owned nothing really, and she paid the bank ever larger sums for a life that felt ever less. But she could borrow more. What was one more debt on top of everything else?

And if there had been a problem, they now had a solution—not an ideal solution, admittedly, but one that was nevertheless workable.

13

A glum introspection took hold of the gathering. Tommy cleaned up the table and then went into the kitchen to make tea.

Though Anna and Terzo could now return to the lives they understood as their real lives, it really meant going back to the smallness of their phones, the only truly individual life free of others, a perfect solitude, thought Anna. She began checking messages and email. Links to articles, memes, news items. Estimates of animals killed in the fires scaled up from half a billion to billions. It was inconceivable it was already over it was foreseeable that most of Australia would become uninhabitable that Australians might become climate refugees in their own land said a visiting climatologist. She wanted to post something cheerful she took a photo of her feet in the new sandals she had bought at Sydney Airport. *New shoes!* she wrote. Oceans were warming at the rate of five atom bombs a second.

And yet as she scrolled and swiped, grew amused or outraged and always more panicked and more anxious, she sensed that the money meant to keep them separate from their mother did no such thing; the money was binding them far more tightly than they wished to be bound to the truth of Francie's failing body. It was, thought Anna, as if her mother's thwarted ghost was beginning to demand some payment in return for being cheated.

14

After leaving Tommy's, she had the Uber drop her off at Willing Brothers in North Hobart. She ordered a pastis on ice, a habit picked up from Meg, and in that little bar she sat by herself, staring into the ice cubes in her tumbler. Finally, she rang Meg to tell her the news, how $100,000 would free her from having to return every second week to Tasmania. She had never liked the island on which she had grown up, the island that as a young woman she felt had threatened to crush all that she wished to be.

Meg said she knew.

Anna said as a young woman she had sought to escape the island as soon as she could but it kept drawing her back like a bad relationship.

Meg said she had heard it all many times, that Anna didn't have to say it.

Anna said I just need to talk, Meg.

Meg said she knew, she knew.

Anna sensed she was trying to tell Meg no less than the story of her life and somewhere at the heart of it, if she could just find it, was the heart of her. Her life was a mystery to her—how could Meg *know* when Anna knew none of it?

Meg said she was sorry, but tomorrow she had to be on site at six-thirty in the morning for a meeting; she had to go.

It surprised Anna and it upset Anna how small her life was each time she tried to tell it, to shape it in order to escape it, how it always came out too quickly as a few dispiriting sentences so easily dismissed.

And when a minute later Meg ended the call, Anna felt alone, abandoned, once more trapped and unfree.

15

Rolling the melting ice around in her glass, Anna knew that everything she had just told Meg, true as it was, was also untrue, that in spite of it all she would return and keep returning and every time she saw her mother an emotion would grip her so violently that it would be all she could do not to shake like a leaf. For as long as it took to rein in that terrible emotion she would stand still at her mother's bed. There were no words for the largeness of it, nor for the completely opposed sense of calm and goodness she would feel after sitting down, holding her mother's hand, listening to her breathe, gazing at the unexpected beauty of her mother's ravaged face.

All this too, Anna felt, was part of a story she was unable to ever satisfactorily tell Meg.

And when these feelings became entangled and confused with her desire to flee, to escape, Anna worried that her idea of love was really no more than an idea of fear: fear of being thought a bad person, fear of being shown incapable of love. Does love have to be publicly demonstrated, she wondered, to make love *love*?

Was all their planning to keep their mother alive, all their fighting for unwarranted medical intervention, all the throwing of their weight around, all their buying in of services, and that very night their ponying up of hundreds of thousands of dollars, not because they didn't feel such things but so *they would not have to feel such things*?

And lifting her tumbler to drain the last of the milky pastis she noticed that a second finger, the smallest of her right hand, had also gone missing.

Heading to her hotel, instead of thinking, instead of feeling, she frantically searched *missing fingers* on her phone. Nothing of relevance. *Missing knee.* Nothing. *Missing ear.* Nothing. She tried *lost* and *disappeared.* Nothing. She felt as if drunk, reaching for a table or chair to steady herself and finding nothing there to hold. She began thumbing a question on Twitter: *Has anyone else noticed body parts going* ... but of course no one would have. That was the point. No one ever saw her. No one ever did. Not even the doctor. Only her possibly demented mother saw Anna not as a thing, a type, but as a suffering human being. Anna deleted the line and swiped to a news feed. Numerous species had vanished forever in the fires as she had been drinking, there weren't even enough bees left, fire smoke was travelling all around the world, a politician was saying they shouldn't waste another word talking about climate change but simply adapt and become more resilient. How did you adapt to your own murder, wondered Anna as she watched a cat video. Was that what was happening? Were they adapting to their own extinction? Was she?

It was late at night and it was perhaps pointless, but what had once destroyed the flow of her days felt increasingly like the only reason she had each day for living. And she turned to the driver, and said that she was no longer going to her hotel, but to take her instead to the hospital.

Davy was sitting in the dark when Anna arrived in the ward, Francie asleep, lips occasionally wordlessly trembling, face occasionally gurning, as if more alive in her dreams than when awake. Davy took out his earbuds, smiled his strange part-lost, part-found, part-up and part-down smile, and they gently hugged. He smelt, as he always did, slightly stale, fetid and damp.

She told him that she liked the calmness sitting with Francie gave her.

Your mind's a garden, Auntie, Davy said. Mine's fucking Aleppo.

He could be funny like that, Davy. He said he had some news. Dana, his girlfriend, was almost seven months pregnant. Dana hadn't wanted anyone to know, because, he said, Dana had mental health issues, being bipolar.

He said this as though somehow he stood outside the vortex of voices, those thrilling, terrifying, vengeful voices, leaping and dancing through his cracked mind; as though, in short, he were sane.

But now Dana was in a good place, she was happy, Davy went on, and they were delighted. They had rung her parents, who lived in far north Queensland, and told them.

Anna asked had they told his father?

Davy's brittle certainty broke. No, he had forgotten. He guessed he would. Would that be a good idea? Yes, he supposed it would. He would do that. Maybe tomorrow.

And with that out of the way, his good humour returned. As far as Davy was concerned—splendidly optimistic, terribly naïve, and in his endearing way sweet Davy—it was all good.

Only Anna wasn't so sure, and she felt for her poor brother, who would have to pick up the pieces when they flew like shrapnel into Tommy's life, as they always did when the voices inevitably returned and Davy fell sick.

Davy found another blue vinyl chair and set it up for Anna to sit next to him at Francie's bedside. Tending to alternate between being catatonic on some new meds or highly talkative, Davy that night was talkative—about the prospective baby, about Dana's health problems, but mostly about Netflix, to which Tommy had lately given them a subscription. Netflix passed the time, Davy said. Anna imagined that being unemployed and unemployable Davy and Dana had a lot of time to pass.

Davy said that they had been on a binge now for nearly two months; they watched everything they could, the TV series were like bedtime fairy tales for adults, and Dana believed they helped the baby's pre-birth mental growth.

But lately he had begun to notice something: they all seemed to operate at the level of a puzzle or a game, some of the newer series even followed the blueprint of games, everything was a beautiful pattern which, once discovered, could be enjoyed and appreciated. He got that. Yo-yos did similar amusing things. Spinning tops angry birds. Several video games of which Anna had never heard. He said he found himself watching the way plot points were neatly tied up and all that, your expectations sort of deliberately dashed or cunningly subverted. The stories began to seem as calculated as algorithms rushing you to a conclusion that could also equally be the beginning of a future return click.

Sure, he got that there were things that were just entertainment. Maybe most things and that's fine, Davy supposed. Only if it didn't mean anything it wasn't great for him. He was soon to be a father and he needed something more. He was mad, maybe, but, still, he needed something more. Maybe being mad he needed it even more.

Because he needed to know what he knew when he was fucking—sorry, Auntie Annie, but she knew what he meant, he continued, what he felt when he was laughing, when he was crying, when the wind blew through the window, when the maggots ate through his brain. Shouldn't stories work towards something that we can't get anywhere else? he said. It wouldn't be enough, sure. But maybe it would be something.

18

The shadows thrown in the night-time ward's half-light were gouging her mother's etched face into things that weren't her mother, thought Anna. From one angle Francie looked masculine, from another, almost like a young woman, and from a third she seemed like nothing human at all, a gargoyle, as if she were not only dead, but had not been living for a very long time.

And this last view shocked Anna so much that for a moment she lost track of what Davy was talking about. Why she was so shocked she could not understand: but it was Francie not as a mother, not as someone subservient to her children's needs, but as something that smelt and made noise and shat and pissed; something, in other words, no different from Anna. She turned to see Davy staring at her, his dark-ringed eyes for once strangely alive and alight.

He was a man in the desert dying of thirst, Davy was saying. He didn't want to be shown a sign that said 'Well'. He wanted water. Where is it? Yes, he continued, perhaps that was the question. Perhaps that was the only question. Shouldn't there be some things that at least ask the question?

Sorry, Anna said, looking down at her phone and turning away.

19

On Instagram thousands of iconic birds—crimson rosellas, black cockatoos, pretty little songbirds—burnt in the fires and blown out to sea only to be washed back up on the beach as countless dead bodies merging into layers of wet black ash. Someone posts elegy for a once beautiful country someone posts extinction event. Someone reposts someone tweets someone texts someone asks what's on your phone?

20

She looked at her nephew.

He just wanted to scream at the screen one question, he was saying. What did it mean?

She looked at her mother.

Something? Everything? Nothing?

She watched Francie's lips as they kept trembling, moving, silently shaping words as beyond the window she talked to the witch and Constantine.

What?

SEVEN

1

Platypuses were in danger of extinction lyre birds were in danger of extinction Venice was flooding *again* a giant dust storm was heading towards Sydney. A south coast town at eight in the morning pitch black except for a sickly red glow when the glow comes you know you have to go, one man says, sirens sounding through the town announcing the fire's imminent arrival. A burnt koala screaming on Facebook she pondered opening Instagram she hated Instagram was she Insta? she couldn't do it she dropped her offending finger from the phone screen onto her chest she felt a troubling absence. In bed, in the darkness. Where a breast and nipple should be she felt nothing.

She ran a finger around the side of her chest. She felt her left breast and then ... *and then* ... nothing. Up, down, a rapid panicked rub back and forth. Nothing!

She went to the bathroom and switched on the hot white bathroom lights. She pulled her singlet off and stood close to the mirror. She turned to her left she turned to her right she turned front on. She stared at herself for a long time.

2

And there it was again: the same simple lack. Once more, no pain, no explanation, just a smearing of things: skin, flesh, memory. What remained?—blurring, neither wound nor body but something else.

Certainly something *had* happened. Or it hadn't. Hard to say perhaps it mattered perhaps it didn't. Two fingers a knee her right breast also now vanished.

Anna had become sufficiently resigned to these disappearances to weigh their consequence first in terms of public display—*would anyone notice?*—and second in the degree of practical difficulty their loss might entail.

As far as she could see, a missing breast on neither count presented insurmountable obstacles. Though she could feel its loss threw her balance slightly, its absence could be hidden in clothes. Summer might present issues but summer was now the least of her problems.

She began to laugh.

She didn't know why she laughed. The lost breast suddenly struck Anna as inexplicably funny. She imagined it on the run, free at last from bras, from being underwired, wireless, pushed up, squeezed in, spanxed, taped and padded; liberated finally from being ogled, grabbed, desired, suckled, mammogrammed, envied, biopsied, derided, drooping, flopping, flailing—*no*, it was at last its own breast, unimpeded by what a body brought to it.

Fuck it, Anna thought, turning away from the mirror. She hoped it was a happy free breast and resolved to temporarily make do with some socks in its place, vowing to see what wonders might abide in the chemists for those who had lost their breast in more traumatic circumstances.

For there were worse things.

It wasn't cancer, for one thing. And for another, after suffering a series of vanishings, Anna no longer viewed them with horror or fear but with a dispassionate, almost detached interest.

The only surprise for her was how little she felt about feeling so little.

3

And so her life was to go on as it ever had. Parts of her would go missing and no one, not even doctors, would ever notice. And if no one noticed did anyone care? And if no one cared why should she? Perhaps, Anna thought, there was a strange comfort in it all, even if she couldn't find the words for whatever that comfort might be. In the following weeks she tried to focus on her mother so as not to think about what had vanished, such thoughts being, she told herself, selfish and egotistical.

And she found a curious equation take hold of her thinking. Perhaps she would no longer keep vanishing if her mother could be kept alive. After all, if Francie proved nothing else it was that what was bad could always be made good, that nature would always bow to will, and that their will would have its way in all things.

Fortified by results, as Terzo put it, they had in those weeks turned to readying the old home for sale. When Anna arrived to help on a Saturday morning she tried to ignore the relentless way Tommy took load after load to the tip making it clear that the house was being emptied and readied to be sold. She concentrated on cleaning rather than disposal, but at each point she came across things that insisted they be kept—a koala-shaped tomato sauce bottle, a cut-glass sugar cruet, the old jam pot in which Francie had once made quince jelly and apricot jam—but ended up also being thrown out.

You remember that smell, Annie? Tommy asked when she showed him the pot. The way she would dollop out great gobs of warm apricot and syrup onto buttered pieces of bread? I can still taste it.

But Anna didn't wish to bring to mind the astonishment of the jam in her mouth, its summer aroma filling the house. The filth and squalor were too shocking. Tommy, who had been visiting his mother most days, seemed not to notice. He swept through the cupboards and drawers as if he were not a stranger, but rather at home, finding several stashes of hidden chocolate, mostly out of date. He laughed as he pointed out mouse droppings marking the short distance from their sanctuary beneath the fridge to the jetsam line under Francie's seat where her food fell and the mice dined.

A h-h-h-whole fucking ecosystem that Francie kept going, Tommy said. Sad to see it go.

Anna said it made her sad to see it.

She couldn't see anything, Tommy said. Her eyesight's terrible and she had no idea what she was living in. She wouldn't let me or anyone clean for her. I guess it was right for her.

But for Anna everything was wrong. The smell, the old people's smell, was wrong. The dust her mother hated and which was everywhere, sometimes in tufts and balls, was wrong. The weariness of fabric and rug, the brokenness of things—a kitchen stool with its rickety leg, the frypan base warped and loose-handled, the exposed wiring of the electric jug; the window that didn't open, the door that wouldn't properly close. The ammoniacal stench of the bathroom. It was difficult to endure. The bed Francie and Horrie had had made after they were married in which they had all been conceived and comforted, on which Horrie had burnt the autumn leaves, now fit only for the tip. The side of the bed that was a pile of used tissues and fetid handkerchiefs. Her mother's cutlery and crockery at best greasy to the touch and often festooned with bits of ingrained food, congealed and reformed into aged, hardened filth. The bitumened arms of the chair in which Francie watched television, the end of so many spilt cups of sweet tea.

It was all wrong, and once emptied, cleaned and set right, no longer a home but a *property*, it sold in a weekend. With what equity was left, plus $75,000 each from Terzo and Anna, a small suburban apartment was hurriedly bought, a carpenter found and, under Terzo's supervision, ramps rapidly erected, rails installed, and the bathroom modified with a sit-down shower.

But, for the first time, the family's will and resources were not enough.

4

Francie's homecoming was put off for a week, and then several more. Recoveries promising much were invariably succeeded by a collapse, infection, ulcer, temporary paralysis of this or that—and on it went and it did not stop. These large setbacks—that's how they talked of them, as something reversible—were, in turn, invariably succeeded by small changes for the better, though each time to a body fundamentally less than before.

And so their mother was shuttled back and forth between the hospital and rehab facilities and hospices and back to hospital, and in hospital from the general ward to the dialysis unit to the general ward and then back to rehab and from there to a hospice and back into hospital, and round and round it went, such that it became a pattern, such that it seemed a way of life and they could each congratulate the other, echoing Terzo, that *life is life!*

But in that time Francie somehow skipped the step between independence and total dependence, abruptly becoming too old, too infirm, too incapable, too frail, too confused, too needy, and, in short, *too much* to live in her own home by herself. Tommy knew it, Anna knew it, and Terzo avoided talking about the fact that she would now never return to living independently. And all that long time the pattern they refused to see showed that Francie was more and more in hospital and, when in hospital, more and more needing full care. No one wished to see—far less say—that Francie was dying and had been dying for a long time.

5

As if all this wasn't enough, a few months earlier—shortly after Anna had pledged $100,000 to help Francie—money had also started vanishing from Anna's home.

It was her way to withdraw five hundred dollars in twenties once a fortnight—old school, she knew—and keep the cash in a drawer in the kitchen. When the little pile of bills started shrinking more quickly than seemed right she began taking note of how much she drew down on the pile for shopping or a night out. And each time she'd notice a note or two extra was gone. And then four or five notes, or even more.

It was Gus.

She knew it. She didn't know why it was Gus she told Meg it wasn't Gus.

Meg said it was Gus it was drugs.

It was just a few dollars it was nothing of the sort, Anna said, Gus wouldn't and didn't it was depression the times toxic masculinity the housing market millennial despair screens solar spots and, in her darker moments, her possible failure as a mother.

Which was the same as saying it was Gus, Meg said, to which Anna replied it wasn't saying that at all when, as they both knew, it was.

6

Soon enough other things began to go missing—two diamond rings, one valuable, the other, given to her by her mother, less so but precious to her nevertheless—as well as a gold necklace and a pair of silver earrings. The vanishings grew more brazen. Her only painting of worth, an early Blackman, went missing, next an antique chair, then her Cartier tank watch, a gift from Gus's father when their marriage had been good. She didn't miss Gus's father she missed the watch.

Gus was less about, by which she meant he was there but not there. He had finished his degree but he had told her he was still *catching up on some subjects*—whatever that meant, for she never asked about it either—and she guessed he was keeping out of her way. He lived like a vampire, staying almost entirely in his room, sleeping in late, eating in the middle of the night.

Anna noticed, though, that after each theft Gus was kinder, sweeter, more considerate, and made an effort to clean up the kitchen or sit and even talk. So there was a sort of incentive in it all for her, for him to lie and she to ignore the theft and pretend he told the truth. In a bizarre way it made their domestic life a little less strained and tense, as though the robberies were a strange but necessary lubricant. But mostly Anna saw less of Gus and of what she saw there also somehow seemed less: less joy, less laughter, less chat.

Less Gus.

7

When Gus was little, a child of no more than six or seven, after her husband left, Anna freelanced from her new Sydney home. In the smallest room in her Leichhardt terrace, a tiny house with the largest mortgage, she set herself up with what were then the necessary tools of her trade—drafting table with its rulers, set squares, and protractors, and jammed in along the opposite wall, a door placed on builders' saws serving as a second table for her assorted drawings. Unable to afford child care, in a distant, strange city with no family support, Gus had to play alone for hours.

She learnt to shut the door of her work room and he not to enter. But after a time he would knock, he would come in, he would have a hundred different stories, some true, most contrived, on how he needed her help with the TV, the toilet, his clothes, food. She attended to them but she could not attend to them in the way Gus wished, which was to say wholeheartedly: with time, with love. No; she was peremptory, keen to show her irritation, humiliating her child for his childishness. She had to impress on him that she would only deal with the TV, the toilet, his clothes and the food as work and not as love, that love ran to a clock, and then it was back to their isolated worlds.

She would shut her door once more, her train of design thought derailed, her small excitement with an idea or problem overrun by an emotion so large there was no word for it. She would know that if she opened the door Gus would be sitting on the floor outside, waiting for her at a time in her life when no one waited for her. Sometimes he slipped messages beneath the door for his mother—pictures of her and him, together. At such times she felt she might shatter. His singular love overwhelmed her, negated her, almost deranged her. She would stand up and sit down. She would stand up and sit down and resolve not to stand up. She would stand up and let him in.

Her feelings for her only child were of an almost unbearable intensity, so strong they would shock her. She understood that she would lay down her life for him. And yet that life was not and could not be lived solely for the child, and there was no other life available to them. She understood that she had done everything a woman in her situation could do for her son and she understood that it was for her son not enough. Only much later did she realise that it was not enough for her either. And yet it was not possible for it to be any other way. It felt only possible for this proud, ambitious woman to be less. Her work and life would at such times become a torture for her and she would hate her son. She understood she had to break something in him for them to go on. There was no other way. Hitting him would have been less cruel. She told him to be a man and after a time, she saw, with the greatest relief and the greatest guilt, that he was.

Sometimes though she would break and beg his forgiveness. Sitting one day in front of her drawing for a shopping centre atrium, a job she had tried to infuse with some originality, some element of design worth, some energy and light, but which was, finally, a shopping centre atrium, she held him tight, and sobbed, and told him she didn't understand why.

He was staring at her, and freeing an arm from her grasp he reached up and stretching out put his hand behind her head, gathering her in as the little hand with the slightest pressure that felt immense traced Anna's still full cheeks, her astonished eyes, her wrinkled brow. There was no judgement in his touch only some knowledge that was for Anna terrifying. She felt herself hopelessly tied, but tied as the weaker one to the stronger. And yet there was a beautiful comfort in the child's measure of her fragility and weakness.

She would set him up in her room with a child's chair and coffee table. She would go back to drawing renovations, school class rooms, corporate office makeovers, while he, in seeming imitation, would quietly draw his buildings, endless variations of what he called home with a tall stick woman and a little stick boy standing outside, smiling. He would bring his pictures to her for her approval, for her attention, but there was only so much she could give him. There was something wrong with it all, something that she felt as a physical pain—a shortness of breath, a tightness of chest, a weakness of body, a growing dizziness—but she also understood the wrongness was not in her but outside of her, infinitely larger than her, and that both she and Gus had to withstand its enormous pressure somehow in order to go on. And she had gone on and Gus, she only now understood, had not.

8

When she thought about it too much she would think . . . except she tried not to think about it too much or at all really, because when she thought about it even a little she was overcome with the most terrible vertigo.

She struggled just to stand.

But one day, after much goading from Meg, when her own conscience as a parent finally got the better of her, she knocked on Gus's bedroom door and walked in, ready to tell him she knew. That, in a way she even understood.

But it had to end.

Only when Gus spun around from his computer, she saw that his nose had vanished.

9

It helped to be busy. And three weeks later—reassured that Francie was regaining strength and coherence, even putting on a little weight—when Anna was invited at the last minute to give a keynote speech at a symposium on sustainable architecture and climate change in Bucharest she decided to accept. Before flying out of Australia to Romania, she withdrew cash, topped up the pile in the kitchen drawer, said goodbye at Gus's door, and flew to Hobart to see Francie.

As her increasingly magical thinking allowed her

to believe that Gus wasn't stealing from her while also believing that something good arose from these disappearances, so too at the hospital, by ignoring the cannulas and drips, the machines, the constant activity of nurses checking, measuring, watching, she was able to believe her mother was not just recovering but returning to good health.

She flew from Hobart to Melbourne and from Melbourne to Singapore, where, twelve hours later, about to board her European flight, a message flashed up on her phone from Tommy.

Mum v sick wthshe bad blood posioning. On last resort antibiotic. Doctors say must end dialysis. Tx

She tapped on Instagram Facebook Twitter it wasn't so easy holding a phone with only two fingers and a thumb she read I'm now seeing live ash blowing down the street. I'm now seeing a tree catch alight. Other than flames barely any visibility at all. We need more people to help defend the town. We are tired, but ok. But we are here! Love, Us 🐾 ♥ It felt like a message out of Budapest in 1956 translated into emoji her two-fingered hand ached she swapped hands she called Tommy.

They've asked the family to come in, he said over the phone.

After the call, she clicked back in order not to think. The power is cut, she read. All roads blocked. Trees down on all tracks, no one to fight it. It's a black holocaust. We're isolated. She could hardly continue flying to the other side of the world if Francie was about to die.

Again, as Terzo used to joke.

10

Abandoning her flight to Bucharest Anna was making her way back through the vast caravan of shops to the airline lounge when Terzo rang. He was just off the phone to their mother's nephrologist who had said in no uncertain terms that there was a point at which dialysis altered from life-saving to life-destroying. He had told Terzo that these new complications meant it was, in his opinion, long past that point. They could not in all good conscience continue with dialysis. Nor did they think another admission to the intensive care unit was appropriate and were recommending instead what they called *comfort care*.

Which means she is to die, Terzo said, his speech reverting to the irritating high white American tone Anna always imagined he used drumming up business. Terzo hissed that he could not believe the specialist's arrogance. Did he think he was fucking God? Did he?

Terzo next argued to the point of near-exhaustion for their mother to live. And when he finally asked Anna—exhausted, overwhelmed, once more defeated Anna—to again press her *sweet and wise* Sydney nephrologist friend to ensure Francie stayed on dialysis, Anna, against her better judgement, agreed.

But when Anna rang the Sydney nephrologist for a second time he was very far from sweet and wise. He sounded vaguely monstrous. The wine vintage from his vineyard, he said, had just been *fucked by my fucking idiot fucking vintner*. It mattered, he muttered, to respect whatever the Hobart renal team was saying. It was not his place to interfere any further.

And with that he hung up.

Anna threw down two double vodka and sodas before texting Terzo the bad news.

An hour later Terzo called. The latest report from the hospital was that Francie's condition had stabilised and she was *out of the danger zone*. Things were looking up, Anna should continue with her trip. Through a contact in a Chinese mining corporation he had been able to speak to the state minister for resources and raise, in a suitably appropriate and appropriately indirect manner, the delicate possibility of the Chinese mining corporation making a generous donation through non-associated entities to party campaign funds. In passing he was also able to mention his mother's precarious condition along with the hospital's intransigent position on dialysis.

And in this way, of connections reaching out to other connections and these connections finding mutually agreeable ways of helping each other, by people who know people speaking to other people, a call was made that same day by the state minister for resources to the state minister for health. The state minister for health spoke to a minder who in turn called the hospital CEO. And in an anonymous hospital corridor, the CEO had a word with the renal team's head, and, once more, something was to be done.

12

Having cancelled her onwards flight to Europe and booked a return flight to Australia, Anna now had to cancel her return flight to Australia and book a new flight to Europe. After a further twenty-seven hours of disjointed flights and layovers she had just checked in to her Bucharest hotel when her phone throbbed in her jacket. It was a message from Tommy.

Instead of opening the text she opened Twitter which she thought she could endure. Photos of ember blizzards. Smoke so thick you couldn't see across a road. Four thousand people with no way out gathered on a beach with the firefighters forming a cordon around to protect them. Sand doesn't burn someone tweeted. It wasn't even mid-morning. Forty-nine Celsius. Ninety-kilometre winds. When the fire trucks sounded their sirens everyone was to get under water. This land so vast, its people driven into the sea. When the red glow came was that all they would have left? She retweeted an article on Renzo Piano she hadn't read.

13

She flicked the app shut, stared at her phone's screen and rather than read Tommy's text she dropped the phone on the bed, went back downstairs and stood outside in the bitter cold under a wet concrete sky. She botted a cigarette from a waiting taxi driver, her first smoke since her teens. It tasted necessary it tasted familiar.

Pointing with the cigarette, she asked the taxi driver about the huge ruin opposite the hotel, a poor pastiche of classical Greek architecture in crumbling ferro concrete with rusting steel reinforcing protruding from unfinished slabs and half-built Doric columns, covered in street art and overgrown with dank weeds.

In halting English, he explained that it was less than fifty years old, one of several scattered around Bucharest, unfinished pet projects of the dictator, for which, after his fall, there was no money either to complete or demolish. No one, he said, knew what to do with them. And so they sat, hideous gigantic grotesqueries, decade after decade, as crumbling enigmas.

It was, Anna thought, the opposite of the ruins of the ancient world, which demanded you imagine them as once having had people living in them; these ruins on the other hand had never been used; they had only ever existed as ruins, they were destroyed before they began. They spoke of some overwhelming lack of humility. There was no beauty about their bloated design: they felt deeply oppressive. She thought of

Albert Speer's theory of ruin value that had so appealed to Hitler, the idea that the power of any epoch lies in its capacity to endure millennia hence as ruins. These thoughts gripped her, and then befuddled her.

I am Syria architect, the taxi driver said. Here, Bucharest: taxi driver.

Anna looked at him. He was good looking, if badly dressed. His cracking black leather coat was too large, scrounged, she supposed.

You think this their past, he said. Maybe it is your future.

Was it an observation? An insult? The truth? Though the cigarette was only half smoked, she took one last drag and threw it into the gutter.

And then she went back upstairs to her room and read the message.

Another stroke. Major. Cpnfoyon serious. T

14

Thereafter: taxis, lounges, terminal trains, travelators, escalators, queues, aircraft and more aircraft, until, finally, the electric doors next to the Hobart Airport luggage carousels opened and she walked out into an improbably blue morning. In the ward she had left seventy-eight hours earlier the morning sun cast a harsh light on an empty bed.

15

Her first thought the worst.

16

Anna heard, not without mixed feelings, a nurse telling her that their mother was now in intensive care making good progress. She pondered the term 'good progress' as she made her way across the hospital. People used words loosely. Of course, she thought in her jet-lagged exhaustion, she keeps dying. But she's never dead.

Such thoughts left her strangely unprepared for the sight of a sheet draped as if over some wire frame that was rather the skeletal figure of her mother—her mother who no longer seemed anything like her mother. Anna called her name. The wretched, emaciated creature lying on its side made neither sound nor movement.

A nurse wheeled in a trolley and in a loud voice cheerily began chatting away to Francie while mixing up a slurry of yoghurt and crushed pills.

It's one long fight, the nurse was saying, but you're a fighter. Isn't that right, Mrs Foley? And reaching under Francie the nurse helped her sit up.

She did this with such an unexpected tenderness that it felt almost wrong to witness so intimate a thing, thought Anna. The nurse seemed not to be revolted, as Anna was, by the decaying animal in the bed. And yet

Anna was her daughter and the nurse a stranger. Why was a nurse allowed this intimacy and not her? How could a stranger possess such compassion when she, a daughter, had none?

But she was, and she did.

Mrs Foley is doing so much better with her swallowing now, the nurse said, sitting Francie up, as if the old woman were her sick child and she her mother. She spooned a mixture of milky meds into Francie's mouth. Aren't we, Mrs Foley?

And scooping up more slurry she raised it to Francie's gaping mouth.

Anna pressed the nurse on how many pills her mother was now taking. The nurse put the yoghurt down and checked the charts at the base of the bed, before saying seventeen. When Anna asked if seventeen was a good number, a safe number, the nurse replied that all the pills were necessary or the doctors wouldn't have prescribed them.

The nurse went back to spooning the slurry of pharmaceuticals into Francie, and Francie, she could see, was concentrating hard, straining every element of her being to keep her head angled, her mouth open. She lapped at the teaspoon like an old dog, the long-wrinkled folds of her throat undulating wildly, feebly, in that necessary labour.

Only when Anna asked her mother if she was okay did Francie look up, her eyes improbably large and bulging as they darted around in their frozen world like two terrified, caged animals.

But there were no words.

Anna watched in horror as her mother's chapped lips made slight movements, plaintive little tremors, like a blind baby bird desperate to be fed.

She can't talk, the nurse said, glancing up. The stroke.

The nurse's smile twitched into a grimace and back to a smile, and Anna saw that her eyes were gleaming. For a moment the two women looked at each other and understood they shared this much. Anna felt the room vibrate and spin around her with an emotion as overwhelming as it was unnameable. And she had to look away, to end that moment, to stop the room vibrating and spinning.

When she looked back to say thank you, an orderly had arrived to take Francie away for a scan and the nurse was gone.

And as Anna waved goodbye to her mother in the corridor and watched the gurney tunnel down another endless corridor, she realised that it would be impossible for either her or the nurse to explain to anyone the strange enormity of that moment. And after a further time that was also no time at all, they would forget that moment completely, they would forget each other, and it would be as if that vast emotion had never possessed either of them and nothing at all had happened.

Perhaps Tommy meant it as consolation but when Anna visited him the next morning on her way to the airport and he said that Francie had had a good life, it irritated her.

Was he saying that women should be put in a box and be happy in that box?

When Tommy said that wasn't what he was saying, Anna asked what was he was saying then? Tommy was unabashed. He said he felt Francie found meaning in what she had.

Anna asked if he meant that their mother should be grateful for being locked away as a housewife? As she heard herself start swearing that wasn't a fucking life, she realised that she was once more trapped in the same argument she had been having with Tommy since they were children. The details always changed, but the root antagonism never did. It astonished her that he had a view as deeply felt as hers and yet entirely the opposite, and which he held with an equal conviction. And in the face of someone who would not be persuaded by her, she did not seek to see the world for a moment as he saw it but instead was simply angry with him that his world was not her world.

Maybe, Anna spat, Tommy read their mother's life not for what it was but to justify his own failure? And she halted, ashamed at what a wretched, nasty woman she was.

Her anger didn't affect Tommy. She remembered this calm obstinacy from their childhood. He asked, what if they were all just in boxes? She in architecture, Terzo in business, him in his painting?

18

And the siblings found themselves, as they had so often over many years, each regarding the other from a distance that only grew every time they met. It baffled them both and served to make her even angrier with her brother.

Anna said her box was a hell of a lot better than Francie's—and so was his. So was Terzo's.

Tommy wasn't sure. Did it really make her feel any better being a partner in her own architectural firm?

Yes, Anna said, yes, it really fucking did thank you for asking, Tommy. And besides their lives weren't boxes but choices, what choice did Francie ever have? She couldn't even tidy her own fucking cupboards.

Still Tommy wouldn't agree as he had never agreed. No, he said, what he saw was a woman who found an outlook that seemed, to him at least, true to who she was and where she found herself. He wasn't recommending it as a way to live. Not at all. But he saw their mother's life as a triumph of her will against the odds: a woman who never allowed her circumstances to reduce her. It wasn't a fair life or the right life. But it was *her* life.

Anna retorted that it wasn't a good life.

What life is? Tommy asked.

Oh for fuck's sake, Anna said. We're free and Francie never was.

And with that she left.

19

But when Francie wanted to die, thought Anna, when she wanted to be in control of what was happening to her body, her daughter, with all her ideas of freedom, of liberation, with all her loving cruelty, finally shoved her back into a prison that even her mother's mighty will couldn't escape.

20

Only after everyone else had accepted that Francie was to live and several more weeks of Francie's silence did she finally—almost miraculously—*get with the program*, as Terzo put it, when he called Anna in triumph.

Her brother told her how that very morning their mother had pulled her frail body into an upright position in her bed and, just like that, asked for a cup of tea. For Terzo, it was as if her incapacity had been no more than childish wilfulness on the part of Francie all along. Faced with the undeniable fact of living she had to accept that the family would not let her die,

Terzo told her, wonder in his voice, as though one more asset-stripped company had been successfully phoenixed.

Can you imagine it? he bubbled away. Sitting up? A cup of bloody tea? After all those weeks of not talking?

21

When Anna returned to Hobart that weekend, greeting her mother as she always did, asking how she was and preparing to answer herself as she had done in recent times, she saw with amazement Francie's scabby lips quivering, her mouth shuddering into that craggy smile, her remaining broken yellow teeth and gold crown slowly revealed, as in a voice no more than a dry croak, she replied, her voice slurred, All the better for seeing you, girl!

22

Everything that was ending was simultaneously starting, all the stories were the same, every night she read on her phone several reassuring tales of the monster Trump from the *New Yorker* and *Vanity Fair* written as if it was news when it wasn't even reality anymore, adult fairy tales that in their rhythms and sameness allowed her to find sleep only to wake more anxious than ever. Below an image Davy had posted of a vampire there was a story of a priest being jailed on the evidence of a former pupil Terzo had always said was wide with the truth. Another priest's lawyer dismissed the oral rape of an altar boy as no more than a plain, vanilla sexual penetration case. How? thought Anna. Two weeks after a fire destroyed a district a second fire swept through, burning all the burnt materials. How was it possible?

EIGHT

1

Her thin, pale lips puttered an approximation of a kiss, the desperate gesture by a body that could no longer even fully coordinate that basic movement of face and lips. What remained was little more than panicked desperation. Anna put a hand on her mother's forearm and yet again it was as if it had magically passed through flesh to grip only bone. There was so little of Francie left that everything appeared to hang off her in loose folds—nightie, rings, skin like washing blown onto a winter tree.

Annie, *girl*, she gasped. It was another half-minute before she had the strength to speak again. She lifted her head off the pillows. Please, she rasped. Please, girl. No more pain.

Anna looked at Francie only held together, or so it seemed to Anna, out of habit and exhaustion. For the first time she was aware of the many scabs on her mother's face, of how dry her skin now was, brittle as charred paper, little more than dust waiting to tear and crumble. It was as if not being allowed to die as a whole her body's components would give up individually—sloughing, flaking, disintegrating—their struggle done. Francie was dry-swallowing, mouth agape, below which her jaw was extended, lightly whiskered with hard curly white hairs.

Anna found a pair of tweezers in Francie's toiletries and with them began plucking her mother's whiskers. Francie, seemingly aware of what she was doing, held her face resolutely, determinedly, stoically, as silent as night, as each hair was pulled; but the tweezers shook and they would not stop shaking.

I've reached the end, Francie murmured. She swallowed, grimaced, reset. I want to go.

Anna waited to hear what her mother might say next. But that was it. Francie's head fell back onto the pillows and her eyes closed, as if exhausted from the effort of those words, from speaking at all.

Francie, poor thing, had confused her ongoing recuperation with dying. She had not realised that at her end there would be no end, just an ongoing delirium of life that was, admittedly, no life. She had not understood her children's resolve that she should live. If she had, she might have feared it more than death itself. Anna continued plucking, but her tweezers shook and no matter how hard she tried she couldn't steady them.

2

As far as Anna knew that was the last day Francie spoke. The evening after the failed attempt at hair-plucking Francie had some sort of mini-stroke and a succession of further mini-strokes over the next week. Those few days of speech came to seem what they were, an oddity, rather than a reprieve. Or, perhaps, Anna later wondered, not the reprieve that Francie had wanted when she summoned what little life-force remained to her to speak, in the hope her children would hear her wishes and having heard them honour them and let her die.

As Francie deteriorated with each new catastrophe, Terzo's resolve that their mother must live only strengthened. Where once he flew to Tasmania only when there was a crisis, he was now there almost every week, sometimes for just a few hours, sometimes a few days. He determinedly educated himself about his mother's treatments and medications, discussing, urging and, when needed, fighting with her carers for different approaches, which one doctor had the misfortune of labelling 'aggressive interference'. Terzo responded that he called it caring enough that their mother might live.

And so their mother continued to live no matter what living might now mean. It began to feel almost a madness perhaps it was madness perhaps they were all in some way insane, thought Anna, as she and Tommy repeated Terzo's nonsense about victory until they too almost believed it or, at the least, refused to consider the alternative. In this spirit of shared derangement they hailed a new series of mini-strokes as a victory of sorts because Francie hadn't died. The cumulative effect, though, was devastating: she was left paralysed down one side. Orderlies began rotating her body hourly to prevent bedsores.

3

Over the following days there was little that Anna could do other than watch over Francie, sometimes sitting with her through the long hours of dialysis—machine whirring, Francie's shrunken face further contorted somewhere between a grim determination and an unending agony that invariably left her mother exhausted.

In that time Anna noticed the nurses frequently talked to her mother as though Francie were not a very ill octogenarian but a young Olympic athlete, whose acts of breathing, swallowing or being rolled over in bed were personal best times, achievements of extraordinary courage and endurance and will.

You're breathing so much better today, Francie, they

might say brightly, or happily tell her how well she'd managed *that roll*, when, in truth, orderlies had man-handled her frail body like a carcass. Or they might extol her swallowing, swallowing being a possible prelude to speech returning and thus a marvel worthy of the most outlandish praise.

And perhaps they were not only comparable feats to those of an Olympian, thought Anna, but even more remarkable. Whether it was this force of character, or the medical care, or just luck, her mother, whilst not really getting any better, yet again stabilised enough that the absence of more decline seemed to her children a triumph in its own right.

Anna counted how many pills Francie was now being daily fed—twenty-one—and when she thought about the pills her mother took it was obvious that while six pills were better than seventeen and seventeen better than twenty-one, what mattered was that twenty-one pills were still better than death. Because anything was better than death, and beating death was really the whole point—the *only* point.

And for that reason Francie would just have to work as hard as she could that day and every day to follow in a future without end. If to live it took Francie working as hard as an Olympic gold medallist to get the whole twenty-one pills down every day, well, that was what it took. If it took living like a dog, well, was that not still living? And, after all, wasn't living preferable to dying?

4

Over the next two months their mother slowly—if only partially—recovered from her strokes, first by moving her torso and then, one by one, her limbs. But speech eluded her. When finally able to use her hands, an alphabet board was given to her with which she was to communicate by using a finger to point to individual letters and in this way to painstakingly spell out words.

Anna would sit by Francie's side jotting down each letter until the meaning became clear, at which point she would repeat the word, and Francie would nod or shake her head depending on what had been communicated or miscommunicated.

were we

Frequently the words were muddled, anagrams that had to be unravelled, or the sentences were incoherent and the meaning difficult, if not impossible to guess, or, worse, weirdly coherent, but meaningless.

eye everywhere

Some made them both laugh when Anna read them out. Francie could not escape the joke but, to her credit, she understood it.

she god give

Mostly her mother would quickly become so exhausted by the effort she would simply drop her hand to her side, turn her head away, such that the gaunt, raptor-like profile—so unlike the plump-faced mother of Anna's memory—was etched onto an upright pillow, and there pass out. Anna would see in her mother's sleeping face a new and wholly inexplicable ferocity, at once a revelation and an accusation.

She leant in to help her mother with the board; it was, as it always was now, unpleasant to get too close. Francie's odour was the smell of decay preserved, as if a bottle had been opened in which a yellowing organism, a frog or lamb foetus long dead, lay preserved in formaldehyde—a scent at once pharmaceutical and mildly faecal. But Anna persisted, with patience and a certain bloody mindedness, forcing her mother back to using the board every moment she was awake, determined her mother once more communicate. The board frustrated Francie, who repeatedly pointed to the same letters.

T. E. L. M. E. G. O.

Anna asked her mother if she meant *tell me go*? But Francie's face made no movement. Her finger shuddered above the letter board, as once again she began jabbing her finger here, here, and here, as Anna sounded each letter out, before pronouncing the group of letters as a possible word.

L—e—t, she said. Let? she asked.

And Francie, Anna thought, seemed to nod. Again Francie's finger jolted and hovered, body and mind seeking to coordinate that most difficult task.

M—e, she said. *Let me*? she asked.

And Francie seemed again to nod, and again began shuddering and jabbing.

185

G—o, she said. *Go? Let me go?* she asked.

Her mother's hand dropped.

Let me go? she asked. Is that what you're asking me?

One side of Francie's partly palsied face flickered, a strange jumpy thing as if a stitch in her lips were being pulled tight and then loosened off, then pulled tight again.

Where, Francie? asked Anna.

And when her mother made no reply, she asked again, Let you go *where*, Francie? Where do you want to *go*?

Anna realised Francie was staring at her.

But you'll get better, Mum, she said, smiling back.

Her mother was staring at her. She was unsure whether it was a look of astonishment or terror.

And life will go on, Anna said.

The letter board dropped to the floor.

The shame of it, thought Anna, only keeps growing.

5

The following day her flight home, departing at twelve-thirty, was delayed because of fire smoke in Sydney, moved to two-fifteen, and then to five-fifty, and finally left at eight fifty-five. On boarding, Anna made a joke about the long wait to the woman seated next to her and the joke became a light bantering conversation.

The woman's name was Lisa Shahn. She was a good deal younger, perhaps in her mid thirties. She had black hair scruffily pulled back into a ponytail, a nose ring, wore Blundstone boots, olive coloured linen culottes and a burgundy knitted jumper. There was about her a dishevelled glamour. She was a scientist who ran a government program to save the orange-bellied parrot. There were fewer than twenty birds left in the wild.

Anna asked if she had managed to stop the birds vanishing, and Lisa Shahn replied that wasn't the point. They probably would vanish. Or they might not. But no, they hadn't managed to stop the vanishing.

The attendant came by with the drinks trolley and after Lisa Shahn bought a gin and tonic Anna thought she might do the same. They raised their little plastic cups to each other.

Can you imagine, said Lisa Shahn, holding her plastic cup to her cabin window and gesturing to the clouds, a bird smaller than this cup making its way out there? They're not really made for it, not like those amazing shearwaters and terns and whimbrels and godwits that fly from the Arctic and Siberia across the planet to Tasmania and back each year, she said. The OBP's just a blinged-up budgie in comparison, a battler.

The evocative description she then gave of how each spring these flying tea cups—as she termed them— migrated from the Australian mainland to Port Davey, one of the remotest parts of Tasmania, resonated at some unexpectedly deep place within Anna. The tiny parrots flew across hundreds of kilometres of wild, open ocean, surviving terrible storms, wind turbines, predators and exhaustion, to return to their birthplace and breed in the Tasmanian wilderness.

And each spring, Lisa Shahn said, there are fewer birds.

6

Lisa Shahn took a sip, put the cup down, and stared out the window, lost in thought.

She abruptly turned, startling Anna. Her eyes were fierce, as if suddenly snapped out of her reverie.

Anna, she said, do you know the story of Mathinna?

This mention of her name so direct and the gaze so intense unsettled Anna. She felt strangely affected by being *seen* she felt many things she hadn't expected to ever feel again.

It was a long time ago, the 1830s or 1840s or something like that, Lisa Shahn said. Mathinna was perhaps the last of the Port Davey people, her father their chieftain. People who had lived there for 40,000 years. The whites stole her from her parents, made her a black princess, a toy, a token, a trophy, and then abandoned her with all her family dead.

Anna felt a confusion rising like a riot, her face a prickle.

Can you believe it? said Lisa Shahn.

Anna dropped her head slightly, momentarily smiled

to herself and then the smile vanished, her lips trans-
forming into something set, and she shook her head.

No, said Lisa Shahn turning away from Anna to
look out her window, no, she couldn't either. Anyway,
Mathinna's people burnt the plains and kept the mosaic
of plains and forest alive, the tiny parrots ate the seeds and
sedges of the wet plains, and Mathinna would have lived
amongst thousands upon thousands of orange-bellied
parrots. But when the Aboriginals lost the war and the
few survivors were taken away the burning stopped,
the forests advanced, the plains began vanishing and the
seeds and sedges with them, and the birds started their
long vanishing also. But nothing ever really *vanishes*.
Does it? Massacring Mathinna's people, the plains, the
seeds and the sedges. The beauty. The birds.

She'd thought a lot about this, Lisa Shahn said.
Her tone changed to something less certain yet more
focused. I mean, *someone* did it, she said. But who? Is
it us?

Her grandmother's family was rounded up in Vilnius
in August 1942 when the Lithuanian police swept
through the house they were hiding in. There were so
many Jews in Vilnius that they called it the Jerusalem of
the north. But they vanished too.

Her grandmother, a child, survived when a policeman
saw her crouched beneath a bed. He turned away and left
the room. But they still took the rest of her family. She
never saw them again. That night a nun came and found

her, perhaps because the policeman told her, perhaps not, she never knew, she was hidden in a convent and survived, and came to Melbourne in 1956.

Anna asked why a Lithuanian policeman would do such a thing but still be part of killing others?

Lisa Shahn ordered two more gin and tonics. Maybe, she said, her grandmother was just another Mathinna.

She stirred her gin and tonic with the plastic swizzle stick, jiggling the ice, took a small sip, and jiggled the ice some more, all the time staring down at the drink.

7

You know, she said as she jiggled, that they nearly established a new Palestine, a Jerusalem of the south, at Port Davey in the late 1930s? The Tasmanian government was going to give the Jews it and all of south west Tasmania for a homeland. Crazy, eh? Anyway, Lisa Shahn said, taking another sip, November is the saddest month. That's what I always think. When the birds make it back from their annual migration. Or they don't. Each year, more don't. And then the few that make it back start dying. Or the few eggs that hatch, well, when those little fledglings die, that's the worst. For me, anyway.

We do everything we can to keep them alive, and yet they keep dying. They keep dying and dying and every year I go back and there are less, so many less that it makes the time when I began, which seemed a crisis then, now look like bloody Eden.

Sometimes she thought the birds did it out of spite, that they willed themselves to death because of their weariness with the world, with the failing efforts of their human saviours. Because the world is so against them.

Anna said she could not help but ask why Lisa kept bothering trying to save them then.

Lisa Shahn replied that maybe it was her own form of spite against a world that didn't care. Or maybe she was like the Lithuanian policeman, just one more mass murderer with a bad conscience. Maybe the birds were her Mathinnas.

And she told Anna how her surname Shahn was a corruption of the Yiddish word *sheyn*, which meant beautiful. How when she was little she thought her family had been killed because they were beautiful. Then she grew up and thought what a ridiculous idea. But now she wondered. Early white explorers described the Aboriginals' camps in the rainforest and tea tree groves around Port Davey as beautiful—*as if sited with an aesthetic eye*. Not *they were*. No. *As if.* She found that funny.

The more she thought about it the more she wondered if maybe that's what humans can't do. Live with beauty. That it's beauty they can't bear. That what was really vanishing wasn't all the birds and fish and animals and plants, but love. Perhaps that's what she was really trying to stop vanishing before it was too late. Sometimes she felt love had dried up like a riverbed in drought.

The love, she murmured, as if trying to turn the word over like a rock in that riverbed to find something underneath. *The love.*

But, Anna thought, looking at Lisa Shahn, there was nothing.

8

It was then that Anna told Lisa Shahn the story of her grandfather who each morning fell to his knees and thanked God for all the beauty in this world, about her dying mother whom they would not let die, how it seemed right but how it felt wrong, and suddenly Anna heard herself telling Lisa Shahn that she was terrified that she'd never lived. That one day she would die and she wouldn't be frightened of dying. She would be frightened, she told Lisa Shahn, 15,000 metres over Bass Strait, that she had never lived. She needed to start again, begin over, *to live*, but it's not given to the old to start again.

9

Later in the flight Anna fell asleep. Dreaming that she was falling through a window she grew beautiful green wings like an orange-bellied parrot's, and as she went to land her wings settled into the fixed form of a roof. At that moment Anna jerked awake as the plane hit the Sydney tarmac. Her arm jolted up seeking balance, an awkwardness amplified by the sight of only a stump at the point of her wrist. Her entire left hand, she realised, had vanished.

Amputation, she said gaily to Lisa Shahn, seeking to hide several overwhelming emotions.

I know it's probably ridiculous, said Lisa Shahn. But I can always do with volunteers at Port Davey to count how many parrots arrive each spring.

And she reached into her backpack and passed over a bent card. Give me a call if you ever want to get away from it all. Amputees specially welcome—you don't need many fingers.

As soon as the seatbelt sign went off Anna stood up and rushed down the aisle to get away lest Lisa Shahn see what she felt—which was no more and no less than terror. For other than Meg and Francie, Lisa Shahn was the only person to have noticed what had vanished.

10

Staring out the taxi window into the late-night Sydney traffic as she headed home from the airport, Anna's thoughts turned to a new vision for a roofing structure of a building she was working on. It would be based on the wings she had flown with in her dream. This soaring structure would, she felt, *liberate the building into the landscape* as she had always hoped. Yes, that was the exact phrase she would use in her presentation to the clients. Once home, she rushed to her study to draw up the idea on her desktop computer.

But her desk was clear and the computer—an expensive top of the line Macintosh with the power to run her CAD software—gone.

She walked back around the house. There was no sign of disturbance or disruption. She knew only Gus could have stolen her computer, but she refused to know it—that is, to hold this idea as part of her reality, as a factor in her life, and in her relations with Gus.

She did not call the police. She refused to allow others to accuse Gus of thieving off his own mother when she talked to them of the vanished computer. Because if she did believe he had stolen her computer, if she did agree with what she refused to allow others to say, then she would have to accept that Gus lied to her—he, her own son, lied to her, his mother.

It was unbearable. Her son had his problems, but Anna refused to believe that he might have lied to her.

And yet in her deepest being she knew he had lied, and that henceforth his lies would be part of their love. And she would lie to others about him, she would lie to agree with him, she would lie for him, she would lie for them both perhaps; she would lie and lie expressing ongoing bewilderment at the strange vanishing of her computer, and in this bizarre, roundabout way offer her son the only solace he might know: that his mother lied also, with him and for him, so that he might not feel any worse than he already did. And really, when Anna thought about it now, was it any worse than the lie in which she and her brother had made their mother complicit and imprisoned her within?

Only it was unclear to Anna if Gus did feel bad about his lies. So much was unclear to her. Was his life, limited and limiting, isolated and isolating, was this the only life the world really offered young men, or was he just lazy? Indulged? A parasite?

She remembered Horrie standing at the open garage roll-a-door, his back turned away from what hung within. The greasy smoke from the autumn leaves he was raking up and burning, before finding Ronnie's body in the shed, writhed around him, felled low by the still, chill winter air. And Anna would think of her father shaking—only that—as the police cars clustered, the ambulance arrived, the neighbours gathered and the priest was called, and in that swirl Horrie stood shaking and shaking, and it was as if her father had already begun to vanish. And she had no answer, though she knew others would have plenty. But she had none, which meant that it was what she had always suspected: her fault.

Anna rolled a joint in her cigarette-rolling machine—a less straightforward task than it might seem having only one hand—and lit it to get her through that evening and the next morning lit another to get her through the day. She had resumed this habit of her youth telling herself it seemed to help. It helped the ache in her fingers, or those that remained. To be frank, she had told Meg when Meg objected to the smell, it helped the ache everywhere. She brushed her remaining hand across her face as if swiping away a fly. To her surprise her jaw was still there. Her nose! Her mouth!

It felt a relief—a considerable relief.

And a little later a little buzzed Anna fell while walking to meet a friend at a Darlinghurst café. She lost a footing on a kerb and dropped like a thing already dead.

She broke her ankle in two places and her forearm in one and she was annoyed, not just because no one at the hospital noticed her missing bits, but because she had certain rules about her life. One was that she didn't get sick. Another was that she refused to surrender to age.

It happened, she told herself, because it happened. She told no one that she had been stoned. Was she ashamed? Well, yes, she was ashamed. But not of being stoned. The joint didn't explain the heaviness of the fall, the weakness of bone, the shocking discovery of fragility when she went to pull herself back up and couldn't.

No, no.

She was ashamed to learn that she was old.

12

The signs, Anna thought, had been blinking red for some time. Her age was already occasionally acknowledged by strangers offering the few courtesies afforded the old: the proffered arm, the vacated seat, the sotto voices she always found insinuating and hateful. She could understand each and every act only as another insult. You were old the moment you accepted the arm or the seat. Or so she lied to herself.

Equally she grew aware that the vividness of being young—the light and the lightness; the ease and the easiness—was no longer hers.

Fuck the young, Anna said.

Nothing belongs to the old, she realised, other than property which you discover too late is worthless. Everything, on the other hand, belongs to the young: the future, for one thing, flesh, both theirs and others, for another. Skin. Hair. And then there is hope, love, belief, ambition, desire, wonder.

She felt dizzy thinking of the things that would never again be hers.

Fuck them all, Anna said, lighting up and preparing to draw down deeply.

13

But something was ebbing like a tide and much felt no longer of consequence. In the bathroom mirror she scarcely recognised the slightly stooped, naked figure, the sad, flabby woman missing a finger, a knee, a breast, and a hand. It would be tragic, Anna thought, if it wasn't so comic. She no longer felt the things that she had so long wished to be rid of: unexpected sexual desires, competitive anguishes, wretched jealousies. An inner world was dwindling and replacing it a lessening— the losses and the loss, the slowing and the slowness. She had been good woman, servile woman, bad woman, angry woman, political woman, passionate woman.

And now she was simply frightened woman.

She had been proud of her body—her fitness, her capacity to outlast others in spin, the way she looked even into her fifties in tight skirts, sleeveless shirts, heels. She had taken pleasure in the weave and thrust of her flesh, the power she felt with it. Coming of age when women were told power was all, she had believed in power. Power repressed, power liberated, power unbound were the holy grail for her as a woman. Now she thought: power is a lie. Power is a trap. Power is an illusion.

Fuck power.

She thought of Lisa Shahn's dark, muzzy hair. She thought of Zoe, ten years her younger, who had survived breast cancer, only to be killed in a hit and run the day after she got the five-year all clear. She had loved Zoe. What had power to say about any of it?

Her last sense of the wonder of things had been Zoe's body; so there, just *there*, in its heave and heft, its immediacy and its endless acceptance and giving of touch, caresses, sounds and smells, all she supposed in order that she might know the same. She never forgot being in Zoe's arms, the incomparable sweetness of their nights together.

Thinking such things, she felt herself to be a dirty old woman. Her lusts and desires were now no more than a cupboard of curios she only very occasionally opened. It always made her smile, and sometimes even laugh. That was me, she would say. That was me!

In reply to an emoji she texted an emoji.

Haha, a friend replied.

Hahaha, Anna texted back.

The friend marked the text with a heart.

The money's neither here nor there, Anna replied. It's in Switzerland.

14

She said nothing about the ongoing thefts, but, finally, Anna felt she had to confront Gus again with his laziness, with his parasitic ways, with what, in sum, she had come to view as his refusal to live. If she were to be completely honest the signs had been apparent for several years.

She liked to think that Gus had been a happy child, a lively if sometimes irritating and occasionally obnoxious teenager. But as he came into manhood—or whatever it was young men came into these days: trouble, confusion, fear, bewilderment, loss, madness, anxiety—instead of quickening with life there seemed about Gus some inexplicable lessening.

He spent more time in his room, took less care of himself, grew dishevelled, even dirty, and seemed to have no interest in his appearance, and the only friends he spoke about were those he met online as gamers. God knows who they were—an Anders Breivik type between penning a white nationalist manifesto and organising a massacre? Convicts in a Chinese gulag forced to game after long days in the mines to gain credits for their gaolers on World of Warcraft?—no, it was too crazy, and for a long time Anna ignored it, she ignored everything and pretended that the problems were not Gus's but hers—an anxiety of expectations, of false ambition, of unrealistic hopes.

Some days Anna could almost believe all was well. She could ignore the thefts and her son's vanishings as he seemed to ignore her own vanishings. Some days Gus even talked to her so sweetly, and he would on occasion be in the kitchen and there would be some unexpected act of kindness—a cup of tea, say, or he would empty the dishwasher without being asked, or he might join her in preparing dinner.

But after a week without any such day and much agonising Anna leant forward on her crutch and asked Gus about her desktop Mac.

He said that he knew nothing about it and she knew he had lied, he lied in such an unconvincing fashion. She asked Gus, did he need money, if he needed money he only had to ask, but Gus never asked. No, he said, he was fine. He just stole and lied and she just agreed.

15

Gus could bring on such confusion in her, and with it a strange fear, as if every time she was with him her world was not real and his—and with it, his refusal to engage, his blatant thievery—somehow was.

She would look at him and think how handsome her boy was, how clever, and be even more confused—why, with all the advantages she had given him, was he not successful? She could not understand it. She could only demand—to no particular effect—that he wash, tidy, that he live within the same borders she did, the same neat blueprint she had drawn and called *family*.

But he wouldn't.

For all his outer show of weakness and failure there was some inner strength and resolve that defeated her every time. His ever more brazen thefts were the final defacement of the image she had tried to build of them as a family. She hated them both when she thought about it this way, the way she just wanted him gone and out of her life, yet the way also that they were hopelessly entangled, the way his failure was hers, a punishment, but what was her crime?

Love seemed to Anna a poor and sentimental word for what held them together. A stupid word. A trite word for something that ached and hurt her so painfully. It was almost as if what bound them was some terrible shared wound, some undoing or unravelling that hurt them both beyond any word, and on occasion would leave her gasping as if she had been hit, in actual pain. For so long she had told a story of her good looking, intelligent son and now his review of her story was in: unbelievable, untrue; so much nonsense.

The truth of Gus was unknown, but its evidence— of a lazy, lying thief—suggested a different story. In her younger days she might have sought to understand it as being about power; one story seeking to prevail over another, as if his determined failure was seeking to prove the hollowness of all her ambition and success.

But now she wondered if it were not more funda-mental: a failure of her imagination. She thought of Gus's nose, of her own finger, knee, breast and hand, which she had never imagined vanishing. And yet they had vanished and were, she now understood, always fated to vanish. Were all her failings the same failing?

She had wanted the prestige of the good woman, the successful mother—as evidenced by her successful or even just normal son. In a sense she had had a grand design for Gus but he had not become it: his life was like the ruins she had seen in Bucharest, strange evocations of the abandoned dreams of dead dictators. Gus: ruin theory as wrecked son.

16

Anna resolved to set a humiliating trap for Gus, by saying if he ever wanted cash he should just let her know, that she always kept a kitty at home, in case of emergencies, in the old music box that sat in the bookcase. In addition to the cash she kept in the kitchen drawer for daily shopping that Gus had been regularly stealing from for several months, she now withdrew $2000 and left it in the music box.

For a few days nothing happened.

Why Anna bothered she wasn't quite sure. She just needed to know without doubt, a final confirmation. She would take money from the music box and return it, so that it looked like it was a fluctuating kitty. In reality she used none of it, and sure enough, after a month, $500 went missing. She topped the cash back up and the strange charade began again: her taking and returning cash from the music box, him stealing, her topping up the sums stolen; he pretending he wasn't stealing, she pretending she was spending the stolen cash.

Her heart could have burst. The trap was meant to humiliate him but it humiliated her. But she had to help her boy. He was twenty-six, lost, without a job, money, prospects, he even seemed to have lost interest in girls, the last girlfriend having been some years before. He wasn't unsure of his gender, he wasn't gay, he wasn't crippled, he wasn't a Rohingya in a refugee camp, he wasn't a woman in Saudi Arabia, or a North Korean of any gender in North Korea. He said he was anxious. What did that mean? His mind seemed addled, he lived in some twilight world of conspiracies and dark forces; there was, he believed, a force that was leading to a great vanishing. He was sure of it; he was frightened of it, it was the one topic about which he still seemed able to muster passion.

Some days she would venture into the dark fug of his room and see his back, his headphoned head silhouetted by a bright screen on which colourful ninjas leapt, soldiers fell, bombs exploded, a world viewed from a gun barrel, a rifle sight, as weaving cross hairs caught another figure—jihadist, troll, ogre, soldier, guerrilla, cyborg—as the central figure was forever condemned to running, leaping, loping, shooting, viewing everything from the point of view of a killer murderer destroyer of all things, everything before his gaze disappearing by his digitally enabled hand into fireballs and explosions.

He was vanishing all that time and she never knew it until the morning Anna knocked once more on his door and entered that dreadful room, with its young man's billy-goat odour, its mess, its terrifying darkness. She was determined to confront him once and for all about the money, the thefts, the Mac, his life.

She called his name and when he turned around from the glow of his laptop she saw that one eye and both ears had vanished. What remained was a mouth and single eye that had somehow floated into the centre of his face and stared mournfully, emptily at her. She heard her phone ringing in the kitchen, fled the bedroom and told no one.

NINE

1

She could hear over the phone his tongue stuck like a castanet on the letter *t*. So, in spite of everything, it *had* happened, Anna thought. She hung up.

2

She needed a moment needed not to think not to feel she opened a news feed. A giant pyro-cumulonimbus had risen seven kilometres above a fire before collapsing into a fire tornado that flipped a fire crew's eight tonne truck killing a firefighter her phone rang, Meg in tears, her brother had called, his town in the Blue Mountains was under ember attack, they were ready to flee, his children were keeping cool in the bath terrified if they had a future. Her brother hadn't known what to say, he was their father and he couldn't tell them they did because he didn't know. He didn't know, and it was killing him, not knowing.

Meg talked, Anna looked at a little girl, not even two, standing alone, dressed in a sleeveless white summer dress with pale blue stripes, one hand holding a partly eaten chocolate chip cookie the other hanging off the rail above the coffin of her father—a firefighter killed in the fires—as though it were her father's trouser hem as though he were still alive to protect her. Meg says goodbye a little girl holds a chocolate chip cookie a politician says when it comes to climate change he doesn't rely on evidence a politician says there's a higher authority when it comes to climate change a politician throws a hang loose shaka *a politician! a politician!* a firefighter texts his mother: *We're overrun by fire. Truck on fire. I love you.*

3

Meg? Anna said finally—but Meg was gone. She called Tommy back she did what she never did she interrupted her brother as he kept stuttering.

Poor, poor Mum, Anna heard herself say over Tommy.

And with that it spilt out.

Not Mum, Tommy abruptly told her. *Terzo.*

Their brother had been out on an early morning bike ride. A truck had somehow hit him at an intersection and dragged him, bike and all, a hundred metres along the road, Tommy said. They think he was dead on impact.

4

The following day, after yet one more emergency flight to Tasmania, Anna and Tommy went to the hospital to tell Francie the devastating news. Led by Terzo, they had refused their mother death only for death to now take Terzo. *The money's neither here nor there. It's in Switzerland.* Looking at Francie that day it was clear to Anna that their mother was not there. But where Francie exactly *was* no one could say. Zurich? Marrakesh? Mars?

The weight of their will, coupled to the formidable technology that will could summon to its aid, had proved too much for their mother's failing organs, too overwhelming for her filling lungs and drowning heart to oppose. Their horrific goodness had multiplied into so many entanglements of tube and torment—dialysis machinery, feeding stations, oxygen intubation, tubes and IV stands festooned with bags full of vital fluids, opioids, antibiotics, supplements, binding Francie to pain. The clacking, ticking, beeping machines counted things that were not life yet refused dying to the poor animal below tethered to their torturous yoke. It was all done out of love—nothing so cruel was possible to emerge out of hate alone—and such a love could only grow and grow, until it had created this: the most terrifying solitude of suffering.

How was it possible to have lost her but still have her? Anna wondered. What remained?

Ceremony, obligation, duty, she told herself. Homage to an idea. Yet every gesture Anna made to her mother now felt devoid of human connection, shorn of any human meaning. The horror she felt at that moment was unspeakable.

Was *this* what she and Terzo had wanted?

Anna didn't know. She only knew that it made breaking the news to Francie both easier, because it was unlikely it would mean anything to her, and harder, because it was unlikely it would mean anything to her.

5

Anna left out details that haunted her. The eerie fire smoke in and out of which Terzo's fellow cyclists saw the tragedy unfold. The truck dragging Terzo and his bike along the road. His broken body. His head caved in, Tommy had been told, like an egg. She told her mother that the funeral would be enormous because Terzo was such a well-respected man.

Francie gripped her daughter's wrist with a strange ferocity, as if seeking to transfer or transmit something, or convey her own hurt, or perhaps hurt her daughter. It was hard to know what this unexpected strength was, thought Anna, or, for that matter, if it was anything. Who could say? It was a moment, and only a moment, and then the old hand fell onto the bed sheet.

6

Terzo had no interest in sailing, far less the sea, yet his funeral, organised by his recently estranged partner, was held in a low-ceilinged, sailing-pennant-festooned function room of a Melbourne yacht club. A listless affair of no more than forty, people clumped like ruined custard. A business colleague spoke briefly; a school friend who said that he had lost touch with Terzo *in recent decades* spoke for too long as if to compensate. The business colleague made a joke about Terzo's company nickname, the Sun King. Behind the friend's head, like two rabbit ears, there sprouted two blue and white pennants. Both said Terzo was good at business and loved bike riding. Both said his death was tragic.

She wasn't sure, Anna said to Tommy after the service. Wasn't his death quick? Wasn't it his life that was tragic? All that cycling—

Tommy seemed not to hear. He started talking about how much Terzo had adored Ronnie. He thought Terzo's whole life was really about trying to impress his dead big brother.

Anna said that was silly, rubbish, it was so long ago, of course, of course, it affected them all—

Terzo knew, Tommy said, his head jerking up, his jaw starting to tremble, about the *p-p-p-p-*

Anna stared at Tommy.

Two words stumbled from his lips, out of the dark into the light. Father Michael, Tommy said. At school.

Her brothers had always presented the abuse at Marist as being something that happened to others. Something that did not happen to their family. She swallowed to rid her mouth of the tarry taste of the fire smoke tang that was strong in the room.

It's not like *w-w-*what you think, Anna. You had to put up with the priests. That's how it was. Ronnie had to put up with Father Michael. Even after Father Michael told Ronnie he was in love with him.

7

She had never known.

She had always known.

8

Maybe there's nothing to know, Tommy said. He couldn't say. He had no evidence. Ronnie treated it as a joke.

She said it must have been very hard for Ronnie to have a priest say that to him when he was only fourteen.

Ronnie wasn't in love with Father Michael, Tommy replied.

She stared at Tommy as if seeing him for the first time.

Ronnie didn't know if he even liked Father Michael. He used to make jokes behind his back. Mick the Prick. But he felt sorry for him. That's what he told Tommy. He pitied him. That's what made it so hard for Ronnie.

Anna went to speak, but Tommy, for once, talked over her.

The way it wasn't, he said, and yet at the same time it was.

She asked if that was why Ronnie—

He said he didn't know. Maybe. Maybe not. Probably. Francie told him there was a note. Horrie found it and burnt it the same day with the garden leaves. He never told Francie what it said. And then he couldn't remember. So who could say?

Before all that, though, Father Michael had grown interested in Terzo. Lost interest, I suppose, in Ronnie. Bored, maybe. And went for his little brother. Ronnie had taught Terzo how to keep out of the priests' way, which to avoid, and Ronnie looked after Terzo, he protected him. Made sure he was safe. And, after—well: Terzo becomes, well, Terzo.

People said anything these days, not every survivor was telling the truth, they exaggerated, not every priest lies, who believes a priest now? Once they could do no wrong, now they could do no right. It was easy to accuse but did he have hard evidence? No, he had no evidence.

All Tommy knew was that he couldn't bear to be anywhere near Father Michael when he came to give the funeral mass for Ronnie.

And suddenly Anna wanted to ask Tommy so many things, the obvious questions, she supposed.

The thing is you want to protect your brother, Tommy said, but you *c-c-c-*

As he stuttered a chain of unspeakable sadnesses abruptly appeared before Anna. So many questions were on the tip of her tongue. But the words were suddenly too heavy, they fell to the floor unsaid. A plain, vanilla case. Perhaps she feared the answers perhaps she knew the answers had she always known?

9

To think she had always felt inferior to Terzo. To think she sought to escape feeling less by imitating the one she believed had more. She sometimes rebelled against Terzo but finally always went with Terzo. She fought with Terzo and yet she adored Terzo: her adoration of Terzo was the root of all her anger with Terzo, perpetually competing with Terzo while painfully aware she could never beat Terzo.

And now this.

Terzo! Terzo! Fuck you Terzo!

No matter Marist and its horrors. No matter that she had matched and in some ways surpassed Terzo. She envied him. Her success no solvent of her envy, she hated herself, and she hated him all the more. No matter his death no matter. She hated him so much at that moment she silently vowed to get off Insta, where in the past she always felt compelled to either love what Terzo was doing or upstage it. Trips, buildings, posing with minor celebrities.

Because Terzo married early she had sought to emulate him by marrying at twenty-two. Her husband's vaguely acknowledged business interests, his composure, so valuable in society, that gift of being able to say nothing but smile in a way that flattered others, these and other trappings of success were but the shadows thrown by his wealthy family. He had the inertia that passes as sensuality and beauty in the young and manifests as something seedy in the old. Her initial love was all-deceiving, she had thought her energy was his, that his indifference to action was merely one more aspect of a languorous charm. He could afford an indifference to wealth that she could not, he could stumble through life because there was a floor beneath him many storeys above the ceiling she hoped to break through.

They had no more children after Gus for no more reason than they had Gus but perhaps, when she looked back on it, she already knew. She often thought that there should have been some tragic moment of demarcation between love and its loss: an affair, a stillbirth, a betrayal or tragedy. There was nothing. Something about her husband negated her love. Her affections, her respect, her curiosity: all dwindled and then disappeared, water in his desert.

No matter, no matter.

Everyone attends to their own affairs in their own way. She left, and he only proved his worthlessness by agreeing with her that separation was for the best. She had needed her husband to be less than her as she was less than Terzo, and after achieving exactly this victory, she despised him for not being more.

It was wasn't was a mistake—but that was that!

No matter.

Terzo was dead and who was Anna now?

10

Propped on her crutch, foot embarrassingly bloated in a moon boot, Anna found herself standing in a circle of Terzo's colleagues from his venture capital firm. There was some conversation about promotions at the firm now Terzo had passed on that immediately changed to conventional platitudes after Anna had shuffled her way in.

An amazing bike rider! said one. Up at five every morning, said another, and straight out the door, the old Sun King told me. I'd believe it!

But soon enough the talk swung from Terzo to the traditional lamentations of venture capitalists. Everyone seemed to relax a little everyone agreed excessive financial regulation red tape green tape red the government *must* incentivise funding *must* support value creation *must* deregulate *must* regulate R&D tax incentives *must* fast-track visas for software engineers *must* get the hell out of business *must! must! must!* And once warmed up and relaxed they talked fin-tech and ag-tech and ed-tech law-tech reg-tech and tech-tech; A rounds and B rounds and down rounds, LPs and floats and phoenixes until finally returning to green tape red so the song cycle could begin again.

And while Anna stood there nodding to every *tech* and *must*, agreeing with what they said as matters of the greatest concern, she didn't know why she agreed because, when all was said and done, it didn't concern her, and she wasn't even sure it mattered to them. And it seemed to Anna listening to them that their words were not words at all but incantations to keep her brother's life away, a spell which, when muttered enough in chorus, allowed them to deceive themselves about the things that were most important to them.

11

But it occurred to Anna as she leant further in, smiling, sagging on her crutch, that no one dared say they were frightened or, unlike Lisa Shahn, risk describing what they loved, they were unable to say that something struck them as beautiful, far less confess that they no longer knew how to talk with their children or their parents and perhaps never had, that they were lost, or alone.

Instead they repeated trivial things out loud in the hope it might make them true. Without this deception, which suddenly seemed to Anna so necessary, they might discover that their own lives were based on some fundamental lie which Terzo's untimely end might otherwise reveal. It was as if everyone knew the suffering that constituted so much of the world yet was equally determined to do nothing about it.

How could it be? thought Anna. That was the mystery: *they knew and they knew and they did nothing.* They could not talk about it and what they talked about was a way of not talking about anything at all with the confidence it actually mattered—or so it seemed to Anna that day at her brother's funeral—as they argued about how finance regulation laws were long overdue being removed from the statute books.

They felt their own judgements absolute and the judgements of others idiocy or wickedness deserving the worst punishment. It was as if everyone had to believe their own story—any story, really—because if they stopped believing there would only be reality left to deal with. No one doubted, or was unsure; every individual was infallible because it was their truth, and so there could be no truth and the world was wrong.

And perhaps it was no surprise that no one could any longer decide what was sickness and what was health, what was living and what was dying, far less know what was good and evil, for they were confident only in the knowledge that if they said it then what they said was right and financial regulatory reform was pressing. In the ensuing madness they could only hurt each other. It was, thought Anna, the one sincere thing they did daily.

12

A young man, his face so barren of feature it put Anna in mind of a hotel key card, came up and introduced himself as Justin, Terzo's cycling partner, offering his condolences.

He told Anna he had been with Terzo when—*well*, he said, it was strange. For a moment he stared blankly, and Anna worried it was the wretched vision she must present—half-crippled, semi-breasted, one-handed—but suddenly he seemed to reboot as if he had found the appropriate information in some remote cloud server. He smiled and resumed talking. He wanted her to know that what people were saying wasn't so, or not so far as he knew, that it was just a terrible accident. People saying he had deliberately ridden into the truck.

Outrageous! He had been there and he didn't believe that! Not Terzo! Why would the Sun King of all people do such a thing?

All Anna could think of were those strange, thin fingers, somehow weak, tortured, grasping the bike's handlebars ever more tightly.

It was true, Justin continued, that when Terzo saw the B-double coming, he just put his head down and rode harder. He could have braked, veered off, thrown himself off the bike. Justin didn't know why Terzo hadn't. But he hadn't. There'd be a hundred reasons. Her brother was daring. He liked to race traffic. He could be reckless, but he always won. Maybe he just misjudged that huge truck because of all the bushfire smoke.

How strange it was, Anna thought, that her brother's fingers were so ugly. Of course, he had them all, which was a sort of a blessing, but still she saw them, and him, shoulders bunching, as the truck drew closer.

It wasn't intentional, Justin was saying, that's all. He was sure of it. People had it wrong. He knew Terzo. Why would anyone do that? No, it was just a terrible accident, he wanted her to know that he witnessed it all and it was just that, a bloody awful tragedy and he was very sorry for her loss. Her brother, like him, loved road cycling. And he thought the family should know that he for one was sure Terzo didn't kill himself.

13

After leaving the funeral on a pretext of being unwell Anna hobbled away from the yacht club as quickly as she could manage. As she made her retreat she thought she noticed something strange about her reflection in a shop window. She ignored it, and kept hobbling. And then in the wide glass of a patisserie above a tray of raspberry friands powdered like Versailles courtesans, she saw it again.

She halted. She turned her head back and forth. It was undeniable. She walked a little further on, stopped at a parked car and looked at her reflection more closely in a side mirror.

Her face had begun dissolving, as if in some awful hallucination. As well as her nose, one eye had now vanished and her remaining eye had somehow drifted into the centre of her forehead. And yet people brushed past her without comment. No one at the funeral had said anything to her about her face, or, for that matter, her lack of a hand. Was it politeness? Was it kindness? Was it terror? Her mind was overrun by other questions. Had this happened at the funeral, or before? Or had it just happened?

Confused, upset, Anna boarded a tram for no real reason than to move away from this latest revelation. She was almost immediately terrified at what the other passengers would say or do. Would a bigot loudly insist that she not sit next to them or, worse, would people, frightened by her face, demand that she be thrown off the tram, perhaps violently if necessary? She brought her legs close together she lowered her head she took up so little space she worried she was her own black hole.

No one said a thing.

She tried to evade eye contact by looking floorward, upward, outward, skyward, anywhere but at the other passengers. But occasionally her glance wandered.

No one took any notice. No one looked up. All were staring at their phones. It was as though the signal was weak but if they could just find the hole in the sky where one bar might be had everything would be okay, as if just out there, about to be delivered, was the message they were all waiting for.

For so long they had been searching, liking, friending and commenting, emojiing and cancelling, unfriending and swiping and scrolling again, thinking they were no more than writing and rewriting their own worlds, while, all the time—sensation by sensation, emotion by emotion, thought by thought, fear on fear, untruth on untruth, feeling by feeling—they were themselves being slowly rewritten into a wholly new kind of human being. How could they have known that they were being erased from the beginning?

And only then did she see: every other person on that tram had one eye only also.

14

That night she caught the last flight to Sydney, Ubered home, and on her way to bed halted when she thought she heard a noise from Gus's room.

She knocked on her son's door. She called his name. There was no noise from inside in reply to her knock, for Gus was always armoured and entombed within his earphones, lit up only by whatever game he was playing on his computer, or whatever social media feeds he was part of, as lost, Anna sometimes would feel, as if he were at the bottom of the deepest ocean.

She remembered how Gus as a child would often cling to her leg. What she would give now for such a moment of affection! But back then she had pushed him away and he had held on, she had pushed and still he held, like a tree in a terrible storm. He had been the sweetest little boy, always playing imaginary games, gentle with others. There was something unguarded about him that frightened Anna. She had tried to kill that unguarded thing. She did this consciously so that others would not hurt him as her brother had been hurt. She pushed and pushed until she won, until the unguarded thing was no more, and he no longer clung to her leg.

She thought about her boy who was there and not there, visible but invisible, daily vanishing a little more. She thought about this and she thought about the unreliability of stubborn words that once you said them several times over and over—*lovelovelove* or *familyfamilyfamily*—ceased to make any sense. They were like an ad for food but not the food itself, she told Gus one night, and Gus said something like I suppose so; that was Gus's way, not to worry about words or things like she did; I suppose, Gus said, but she just couldn't *suppose* anything any longer. And yet it's not true to say Gus was careless about words. He never said stupid things or things that he didn't believe, while she, to the contrary, said so many stupid things thinking that somehow made them serious and that naming her feelings made them genuine. Now she wondered if it didn't just make them false. They say you should name things to know them. But sometimes Anna wondered if there wasn't more wisdom in *not* naming anything you truly feel, so that you might keep feeling it. Every name fixes something to the cross, stops it mid-flight; every name, thought Anna, is a bullet seeking a target to kill.

Gus, even as a child, would never say he loved her unless she made him, and then he would laugh as he said it, as though the whole idea were a trivial joke, unequal to what they were. As he grew up he would say that he cared about her, that he liked her, that he felt happy being with her; that above all he found a great peace in her company. For a long time she was offended he wouldn't say he loved her unless she compelled him to say it, to repeat her words, an oath he thought was funny precisely because it was false and insincere. For too long, really, Anna now thought, she had been offended, and beyond offence, angry. For perhaps twenty years she had felt there was something wrong between them because he would not use those words. But what he said he meant. And perhaps what he meant was something stronger than love, something more complex, something unsayable.

<h2 style="text-align:center">15</h2>

She waited a moment or two and then hobbled in on her crutch. The room was darkened, fetid, the only illumination the vivid light of a war game on Gus's computer screen; a place of almost complete sensory deprivation other than that one source of stimulation, a perennial burning bush in that strangely drowned underwater world.

Gus swivelled around in his seat and for a moment she thought she could see or had seen or perhaps just momentarily registered some anguish on his face. But it was only a moment. For his lips and single eye—the last of his face—had now also vanished, and she realised that even if he wished to express something it was impossible for him to show any emotion.

What remained had become as inscrutable and unknowable as some piece of classical statuary desecrated by rampaging early Christians when that world had also vanished, sans colour, nostrils, lips, pupils, all smote and lost forever. It was as though Gus's face had slid off his head like dinner off a plate.

Perhaps she gasped. Perhaps she was struck silent. Later, she couldn't say. It was hard to remember anything other than that mournful oval staring at her, still somehow Gus with its shape and hair, with its melancholy movements, still somehow human with its recognition of her and its suggestion of some indefinable and now unknowable sadness fire-lit by bombs exploding on the screen.

She went to hug him, she went to hold her son to her body and never let him go, and as he rose from his chair she saw one of his arms had also vanished. She didn't feel shocked at its absence but only sad that he would never again hold her as he once had.

Never mind she told herself, she could hold him; yes, she thought, that was still possible. But really, truthfully, nothing normal was any longer possible, thought Anna. She dropped her crutch, her arms encircling the growing emptiness that was her life. And as she cradled him, as he looked up at her with that terrifying empty visage, a likeness of feature now only inadequately suggested on that sad oval by stubble and a strange single lensed eyeglass framing featureless flesh, she wasn't horrified, but she felt unexpectedly moved, even fascinated—where on earth had he found such an odd-looking eyeglass?—and she gazed back at his emptiness as though a veil had been torn away.

Was it an expression of remorse, or hate marking the remnants of his face?—or of a complete and utter failure that was hers and hers alone?

16

Meg brightened. She was sitting with Anna in the ochre haze of a shadowless early evening in a Surry Hills café, drinking rosé. The bushfire smoke obscured the city and soured everything including Anna's taste for the wine, and it was bizarre for it to be so late in the day and for there to be no shadows because of the filthy light and no sense of impending dusk.

Bizarre, yet normal.

Meg was talking of how once she was passing the house of an old friend—and by old she meant this woman had been old back when Meg was young, and the old lady was fun, and kind. She was a chain-smoking poet and at the time she, Meg, wanted to be a poet.

Anna was staring at Meg, eye to eye, struck dumb, unable to voice what was so obvious: Meg, just like her, now had only one eye, although her eye was not centred but remained on the left-hand side of her face framed by a tortoiseshell monocle. Why was Meg not also similarly shocked by Anna's single eye?

Meg—, she started wanted tried, Meg! Please! We need . . . *we must talk.*

Tucking one leg under the other, Meg went on

about how the old lady had cooked exotic dishes like coq au vin.

And where once Anna had felt with Meg free and able to talk about all things—the most secret, the most trivial, the most strange—now she felt their opposite, that nothing could be shared, that she was mute and unfree within her own silence, and Meg's one leg folded beneath the other seemed like a careless habit and what Anna had once found so attractive now irritated and even repelled her.

She served far too much sherry, Meg said, and talked of being at Cambridge with Ted Hughes. Can you imagine it? All this was very exotic in eighties' Wollongong. She was a lovely old woman and she lived in an old cottage with a great big pepper tree in the front yard. And then she died.

Meg, Anna said. Meg, can you see me?

Of course I can see you, said Meg. She took the monocle from her eye and holding it up between them, turning it back and forth as if it were something precious, she smiled. Cute, eh? You were always at me not to be self-conscious about glasses and now I have this monocle everything is so much clearer.

Anna stared into Meg's dark eye, a hazel kaleidoscope that had once undone Anna and now terrified her. She asked Meg if she might put her leg down, saying it looked a tad childish.

Meg dropped her leg, and continued with her tale.

Many years later Meg was driving by the cottage and she noticed the pepper tree had been felled, and that magical little cottage with its laughter and its mystery and magic and joy was now just another house. And she was overcome with the most terrible sadness. The old lady was gone, the magic was gone, and what did her life mean because it seemed to mean nothing, or as much as the pepper tree, something that could simply vanish and with it everything that gave life its meaning.

Meg, Anna said. Please, look. Can't you see?

And that day, Meg said, drawing her leg back up and under, as she sat there in her car, staring up at the cottage, she could find no answer. She had thought that cottage, those days, that coq au vin, were the start of something great in her life. But they weren't, Meg continued. A terrible hole opened up in her stomach like a hunger that might eat her up, that could swallow her from inside out. She became an engineer.

You never know at the beginning of things that this is also their end, Meg said, that what vanishes is not just them but you.

17

Life went on more or less as it mostly goes on, thought Anna. In the great cities there were more pressing matters such as whether the mass transit continued to run or the garbage was picked up; whether wages were paid or wages were spent; there were so many things to be bought and sold and retailed along with them the idea of unnecessary things being necessary, even fundamental, and the great circus rolled on even when other life stopped or just grew too grotesque and terrifying to contemplate.

Sometimes in passing or when people were in their cups a story would come up of another adult son reduced to a hand, a gesture, a shadow, but it was, as Meg called it, *a buzz-killer*, and the chat would sweep like a river around and over it and move on to sunnier valleys.

It began to seem to Anna that the only thing worse than the world not taking note was perversely when it did, making the vanishings a small story buried in some alternative news feed as if, at best, it were simply the province of cranks or social media conspiracies, or, at worst, worthiness. It was just common sense to see it wasn't right, Anna told Meg, but, as Meg pointed out, everything wrong was now common sense.

For a time Anna tried to talk about it, only the more she kept bringing it up the more other people would seek to be distracted by other subjects. From the moment she mentioned a vanished nose or ear lobe, other people would start talking about politics or Netflix or TikTok. The more preoccupied this would make her with her subject the more preoccupied they became with theirs. She would talk about missing eyes and they would talk about the prime minister. She would talk about vanishing sons and they would talk about mortgage stress. No one knew how to say what was right in front of where their noses had once been.

Nowhere could Anna see evidence of a world wanting to take the matter seriously. Perhaps the more the essential world vanished the more people needed to fixate on the inessential world.

What else did you expect? Meg said. Meg annoyed her more and more.

Of course, people still talked, but, in some fundamental way Anna didn't understand, they weren't strictly conversations at all, but non-conversations in which each person talked ever more insistently to avoid the possibility of a conversation ever happening.

In any case it was summer, and summer never really ended anymore nor really began, it was just hot or intolerably hot, and the bars and restaurants and cafés were full and happy, and while *the vanishings*, as they were now sometimes called, began to be talked about a little it was only a little. There was only so much to be said and every day something more ridiculous, more tragic, more laughable, more *newsworthy* had occurred—a political scandal, a child's murder, a man's penis bitten off by an angry lover. Some people worried. But the reality was most didn't, or didn't enough.

And when the first famines began, they were elsewhere, and the growing numbers of wars were elsewhere, the atrocities and horrors were elsewhere, and elsewhere is always the fault of others, and others were always less able and more stupid than them, and so they didn't worry too much about these things either, nor were they overly concerned when refugees fleeing these horrors were turned away from their borders or incarcerated because, with their two eyes and noses, it was clear they weren't really like them at all, but freaks.

Maybe, Anna told herself, the vanishings were not so bad. It could even be argued that they weren't really a problem at all, but a natural adjustment, a process that simply would take society some time to understand and manage.

And maybe they were, and even when it began to be reported that as well as eyes and limbs and extremities, sons had started vanishing, the abnormal had by then long been normal.

A few tried to publicly draw attention to the vanishings, some mounted violent protests, a handful indulged in pointless and terrible acts of terrorism, but all these things, even such outrages, were, finally, third-tier news that was of little concern to most and too depressing for all, and there were still plenty of happy things, or at least things that people believed made them happy. But Anna found herself recalling Terzo's funeral, certain details of which haunted her: the low white ceiling with its symmetrical constellations of harsh downlights, the jaunty pennants, the immense emptiness she had felt overwhelming her.

It was as if words were now a wall between people rather than a bridge, and if you could just build the wall high enough no one would see the growing desert of the vanished on the other side. It was as though everyone was using words to avoid using words for what words were used for. She began wondering if the very reason for words had also vanished, and what she heard now when people talked, when Meg talked, weren't words so much as a drone, that same drone Tommy was always on about.

For she had begun hearing it too: at Terzo's funeral, in cafés, on the street; penetrating rooms even when all doors and windows were closed, rising up through her bed and pillow even when she slept, she could feel it drilling down into her very teeth nerves while she dreamt. But Meg would merely grubble something in reply if Anna asked her if she heard anything for Meg didn't care and never heard.

Anna saw less and less of Meg.

There was, in any case, less and less of Meg to see; one night Anna sat up in bed, having prepared the phrase, Meg, I think I have fallen out of love with you. Like the good minimalist architect she was, the phrase, she felt, was elegant, strong and sufficient without the need for elaboration. But like Gus before her, a little more of Meg was dissolving with each passing day, fingers hands limbs vanishing, and Meg neither seeing it in herself nor seeming to notice it in others, and when Anna went to touch her shoulder there was nothing.

Anna? grubbled Meg.

Nothing, replied Anna. Nothing at all.

For periods of time Anna was able to forget about it, but then it would be back, a high-pitched noise, sometimes a beeping, sometimes a pulsing, sometimes a more consistent shrill whine, at other times close to an inhuman shriek. It was like a pain or a loss. Perhaps it was pain, the only pain, and for as long as it endured nothing else was possible. Without discussion, without comment, she realised she no longer slept with Meg. Worse, she preferred sleeping alone, reading her phone.

19

She googled 'Jerusalem of the south' and 'Port Davey'. Through archives and reviews and histories and academic articles she began to piece together the story.

A Latvian orthodox Jew, Isaac Steinberg, foreseeing the Holocaust, had sought to find a new home for the Jews of the world at the moment of their greatest peril. One-time commissar for social justice under Lenin's first government, known as the Butcher of Moscow, later imprisoned by Lenin, Steinberg escaped and ended up leading a breakaway from the Zionist movement, trying to get land for his Jewish homeland in the new world in the late nineteen-thirties. Madagascar. Ethiopia. North west Australia. But only the Tasmanians considered giving him the land he needed for his new Palestine: Port Davey and the surrounding uninhabited south west quarter of their island.

How many might have been saved?

Steinberg warned of what was coming in Europe. But people couldn't see what Steinberg could see. And people couldn't believe that they could save the world. By 1942 not even Steinberg believed it.

But one lone goy did.

His name was Critchley Parker. On an arthritic website that creaked page to page while loading, Anna found the text of a talk given about him in 2009 in the papers and proceedings of the Tasmanian Historical Society.

Parker had fallen in love with a married Jewish woman in Melbourne who was a supporter of Steinberg. In April 1942, just as the summer of the great slaughter began in Europe, that skinny young man, chronically unsuited in temperament, health, experience and back-ground, to surviving in such a wildland, found himself exploring Port Davey and beyond, an almost unknown and uninhabited country. As the business of genocide was being rendered industrial with the advent of mass Zyklon B gassing in Europe, Critchley Parker was planning the great capital of world Jewry in the home of the orange-bellied parrot.

He did it to impress the Melbourne socialite, because somehow his forlorn love and her crusade had become one. And he died alone out there. You could almost say, the author wrote, that he died from too much love. Maybe it was stupid. Maybe it was pointless.

But Anna was moved: *he did it.*

It somehow seemed a victory.

Anna scrolled to the bottom of the document. The author was described as an associate professor of zoology at the University of Tasmania, specialising in avian extinctions.

Her name was Lisa Shahn.

When the orange-bellied parrots returned the following spring, some tin prospectors found a slimy skeleton in a sleeping bag. It was Critchley Parker, his tent long ago blown away, and alongside his corpse was a diary of his dreams and plans for the capital of world Jewry, to be designed by Le Corbusier.

Who else? he had written.

By then it was the northern winter. Three-quarters of Europe's Jews who were to perish in the Holocaust, Lisa Shahn's family among them, were already dead.

20

When Anna's bones finally healed she didn't return to her practice of running daily. Didn't go back to the gym. She observed with indifference her body refusing to rejuvenate, to grow hard and taut, to tighten and strengthen. What did she care if she were flabby flesh or haggard gristle? She had learnt that people were remarkably unobservant, thinking they were seeing the same person when that person was vanishing before them. Bit by bit they dissolved and yet no one seemed to notice. The more things changed the harder people stared into their screens, living elsewhere, the real world now no more than the simulacrum of the screen world, their real lives the shadow of their online lives. The more people vanished the more they asserted themselves online as if in some grotesque equation or transfer. Meme artist, influencer, blogger, online memoirist. She wondered if the more they were there the less they were here? Did she know?

No, thought Anna, she didn't know; she knew nothing, but it seemed to her at times that not only were people not seeing but perhaps—and it was this that struck her as more frightening than anything—*they did not want to see.*

And above all things, she wanted to see.

She wished to once more observe the world not as people said it was, but *as it is.* She wanted to be attentive to this *is*, not panicked by what wasn't. She needed to precisely know the world as it presented itself to her. And if it revealed a bruised, damaged universe, still, perhaps there would be in the very wound some hope. These things seemed suddenly clear to her. But less clear was how to achieve them. She checked WhatsApp she checked Insta. A charred rainbow lorikeet halted her scrolling.

21

Set amidst a tidal rind of wet soot on a beach, the bird was burnt and drowned, red beak bright, blue crown vivid, green and yellow and orange plumage kaleidoscoping into oily burnt leaves and black bark. Its one open eye stared up at Anna in terrifying judgement.

It saw!

It saw and it saw!

Fear felt close. Wasn't that what everyone was saying now? Summer was frightening. Smoke was frightening. Having children was frightening. Living in the forest was frightening. Choking in the cities was frightening. Today was frightening. Tomorrow was terrifying, if we made it that far.

22

The following day she found Lisa Shahn's card in her coat pocket. She balled it in her hand and was about to throw it away when she stopped. She flattened the card back out. She stared at it for some time. She remembered her muzzy hair, the way she said, *Anna*, how intensely she had looked at her, and, above all, how she had noticed her missing hand. And she picked up her phone and called Lisa Shahn. Why? She didn't really know. The line went through to voicemail. She hung up without leaving a message. She put the card in a small woven grass basket she kept for keys and there it stayed for some weeks until one day, annoyed with the growing mound of junk in the key basket, she went to throw it out. And just before she did, she halted, looked, thought, and once more dialled Lisa Shahn's number.

This time Lisa Shahn answered.

Anna had no idea what she would say to Lisa Shahn as she heard herself speaking slowly and confidently, explaining that she was the woman on the plane, the one who had lost her hand and who now just might be losing her head. She had seen a picture of a dead charred rainbow lorikeet, such a beautiful bird, and it had broken her heart. She hoped it wasn't presumptuous, but she had a question.

TEN

1

Degeneration regeneration decay. Lasix Zithromax Warfarin Nexium Fentanyl. Tales told by idiots were where what doctors making less and less sense who came next who?

Francie could die or she might not *yes* she could be or had been *yes* she was doing well *yes* except for the fact that she was doing badly. Yes yes yes no *really?* So much knowledge so little wisdom. The doctors were very pleased with how well she was responding to this or that she didn't respond at all. New procedures old vanities alternative treatment was really no treatment at all many thanks no yes not at all. *We could always try.* Yes no maybe. Hope as long as you didn't buy the despair.

Sometimes it seemed, thought Anna, no more than a program of cruelty, its only interesting feature the way each misstep always ratcheted up Francie's misery.

And at the heart of the mystery that was the medical system the greatest perversity of all: the kindness of those who worked within it. The orderlies so patient, the nurses infinitely gentle, the woman who served Francie the meals she now rarely ate so tender. A young Sri Lankan woman doctor who cared.

And yet all their care and their kindness were for Francie only so much more suffering. Anna sometimes felt that to inflict such torment on a sentient creature in any other sphere of life would be considered criminally psychopathic and merit heavy punishment.

And this invisible crime flourished and was only possible, Anna realised, because of a lie. And that lie was one they—children, doctors, nurses—all encouraged. The lie was that postponing death was life. That wicked lie had now imprisoned Francie in a solitude more absolute and perfect and terrifying than any prison cell.

Anna wondered if this lie, more than any pathology, was why Francie no longer communicated. Why would she when no one listened? Why when all her words and wishes were turned against her? Everything was framed by the lie—from eating which would help her get better to taking her meds which would ensure she didn't die to the next procedure which was always going to get her back on her feet.

The lie began in the pity—the pity she and Terzo had shared with the doctors. Such pity was in its way no more than the expression of the most terrible vanity on all their parts. After all, what was pity, if not sorrow grounded in the illusion of power? And what was power? Nothing, thought Anna. Nothing at all. They could not save Francie but they could make her suffer. That was the only power they had.

2

Anna stood next to the bed where her mother lay recovering from several hours of dialysis, and she saw the immense damage done in that short time since she had last visited. Everything now seemed to hurt Francie. She even had to battle her breathing, panting shallowly to evade the tickle that would lead to convulsions of coughing so extreme they would often end with her vomiting green bile. So weak was she that the moment her coughing ceased she would fall asleep, and asleep, even more terrifyingly, her breathing would sometimes stop altogether.

It was as if they, her children, were the puppeteers who could keep the illusion of life alive and the illusion was even more necessary than Francie, now no more than their marionette suspended by tubes that ran from machines and their life-condemning fluids above to various shunts, catheters and orifices below.

She is a great character, your mother, the young Sri Lankan doctor said one day.

Anna had never thought of Francie in those terms,

or, for that matter, any terms outside of her home and her family, and it shocked her to think of her mother as somehow being an adult independent of them and their needs, whom others enjoyed for her company, her character, her fully realised and hitherto invisible, unrecognised human qualities.

The young Sri Lankan doctor said she was beginning to understand what an old doctor had told her when she was a medical student; that the measure of us is not what we say or think, but what we are when we are tested by suffering.

And of Francie's suffering there was now no end. Caught between her body's desire to die and her remaining children's determination that it live, Francie was being tested in extremis.

3

Anna flew back to Sydney, Ubered home, and once there she knocked on Gus's door. Hearing no reply, she limped into his bedroom.

In the darkness the computer screen threw a flickering light. Gus was nowhere to be seen, but she noticed a gun sight moving on the screen, tracking an animal in flight that transformed into a bird. Below the screen she saw a one-handed gaming controller, slick black with use, and wrapped around it three fingers and a thumb moving in and out of shadows.

But there was, Anna realised with a rising nausea, no hand. There was no arm, no body. She anxiously scanned the room for some other remnant of her boy. There was none. There was no Gus.

With her remaining hand she reached out and steadied herself against the door frame. She gasped several times, fighting for air. She stood there for some moments as if resting, a small woman in the dark.

The gun sight's gaze was fixed on a doomed world running, leaping, loping, flying, seeking to escape the next bullet, missile, apocalypse, the old world exploding into nothing while below the screen, Anna now understood, was all that remained of her son—three fingers and a thumb—jerking back and forth like a frog leg in a high school experiment.

The gun sight ominously roamed the screen searching for the poor fleeing bird while, grasping the controller, Gus's remnant hand slunk back and forth replicating the gun sight's movements. It was hard for Anna to know if it was Gus's fingers moving the controller or the controller moving Gus's fingers, as though his jerking fingers and thumb were no more than a dissolving avatar of the real thing on the screen, a digital gun sight animating all that was left of her beautiful baby boy.

A scream gathered in her throat, her mouth fell open, but from it there sprang only a collapsing, endless space into which she was terrified she now might disappear. It was as if she wanted to vomit something but there was nothing something everything nothing. Even the possibility of screaming had vanished. And without a word—as if any words, she thought, could penetrate such a horror—she left the room and shut the door quietly behind her.

4

Her son was always here and not here, you could say, thought Anna. More and more he was not here. He was not there. He was not in Switzerland. He was not anywhere.

5

It was okay, said the nurse, it was always okay, the worse things became the more okay it always got, only Francie had now lost her ability to swallow and would have to be sustained by a nutritionally enhanced fluid that was to be fed her via a tube inserted down her throat.

Three nurses came to Francie's bed half an hour after the doctor left his instructions. Amidst assurances that all would go well Anna was asked to leave. When she returned Francie's mouth was strangely slack and out of her nose ran a plastic tube that looped up to an IV stand, off which sagged a bag of yellow fluid.

Francie turned to face Anna as if she had been caught in some forbidden act, as though she were guilty of living. Her cheeks, normally powdery and dry, were glistening, the sides of her eyes a filigree of silvered wrinkles, the first tears Anna had seen on her mother's face since the day they buried Ronnie.

6

She was disintegrating before their eyes. Almost a panic came upon Anna, as she insisted, demanded, begged, borrowed, and bought anything that might halt their mother's decline. Various contraptions began enshrouding Francie's body to stop it breaking down further—a mattress regulated by a computer that routinely inflated and deflated in separate zones to stimulate circulation and prevent bedsores, hoops to prevent sheets from rubbing a body now so frail sheets threatened it.

Each time Anna saw her mother now the shock was so great that something would lurch wildly inside her. Sometimes she would almost lose her balance and to steady herself she would have to grab the blue vinyl armchair or push her back into a wall. For each visit was to meet a different woman, each woman a further diminished version of her mother and each woman less like the last woman, each mother Anna greeted less and less her mother.

Once steadied, Anna would step forward, stroke her mother's face and begin talking so calmly and gently that her voice seemed unrecognisable as her own, using the same words that are uttered by every visitor to such beds in such places at such times, the same platitudes, the same small news—the same determined babbling into the void.

She rubbed her mother's bony knuckles. Francie made some hoarse sounds, and Anna leant in to see if she might decipher them, her remnant fingers softly riffling the loose wrinkles of her mother's hand.

But it wasn't possible. It hadn't been possible since Francie had asked for the last rites. It wasn't even possible to know what she was thinking. Her arms and hands no longer obeyed her body enough to use the alphabet board. It was only possible to know that they could not communicate, that Francie was lost somewhere far away and would not return.

There was no coming back.

Once when Anna arrived it was to witness Francie waking with terrible pain, her bony limbs jack-knifing like those of a swotted insect, her face contorted in a rictus of agony. On another afternoon, an eyelid refused to open, and though the doctors said all was well, that she was stable, that she was comfortable, Francie made slurring sounds of distress, the most horrible animal noises halfway between a bellow and a bray. But after only a few noises she would grow exhausted, stop, fall asleep, only to wake a minute or two later and begin braying her agony once more. It was grotesque, unhuman, so animal that Anna wanted to flee.

But she didn't. She thought of Gus, she thought of how much she longed to hold him.

And Anna took hold of her mother and slowly rocked her as if she were no longer her mother but her baby and she held her mother close because that was all she could do, because the moment she let go she feared everything that would follow as it had followed with Ronnie, as it followed with Horrie, as it followed with Terzo, as it was following now with Gus.

In a visitors' notebook on Francie's bedside table Tommy left sentimental quotes from poems and songs. They irritated Anna, perhaps because the triteness of the sentiments seemed so out of proportion with the enormity of what had befallen their mother. But when she read them she sometimes cried, at her mother's fragility, at her own weakness in being so moved, at how great sorrow perhaps only allows banal responses. And reading the quotes she would even half-believe them, a net in which she became entangled as her thoughts became entrapped in the logic of words.

But in that child's notebook her mother had once filled with indecipherable hieroglyphics no logic prevailed— and only there, thought Anna, in that complete loss of communicable meaning, could be seen clearly her mother's tragedy. Even one correctly drawn letter of the alphabet would have made of that tragedy something less, something not so painful, something untrue.

Her first memory: climbing into bed with her mother, rolling into her scent and great warmth, as the rain fell on the tin roof and thrashed the window, and her world was those arms, that smell and warmth, as the noise of the world fell away.

Once more, Anna climbed into bed with her mother. Her smells no longer repulsive, her sounds no longer frightening, she held her mother close, she wove her hand under the precariously placed IV lines and, as softly and gently as she could, stroked the loose rag of flesh that was her mother's arm, black and blue bruised from too many months of needles and cannulas. She was conscious of her own loneliness and of her mother's loneliness and of how holding Francie did not end that loneliness for either of them.

Anna held her mother but her mother did not hold her. Her mother had no power to stop anyone draping their arms over her, forcing her into an embrace. No power to resist nor to welcome. That was what they had made of her, thought Anna: a woman not a woman, a human not human, love unable to love.

She felt her mother not as she once had, as a vibrant force of flesh and opinion and certainty, but as unruly bones pushing out everywhere; yes, thought Anna, just those sticks and a gathering emptiness within.

She felt that for so long as she held her mother both could bear the pain together and help the other exist in the gathering emptiness. That if they could not banish the darkness they could, at least, each offer the other the solace of touch. That much, she thought. It gave them both peace for a short time, and a comfort they desperately needed, soldiers in a foxhole waiting for the next bombardment. And she was grateful.

At some point, realising late evening had come, Anna got out of bed, and once she had settled her mother, left.

8

Outside it was a full moon. She found herself following the river up to the Cenotaph, and from there walking over to the Domain, once the great colonial park of the town, now a sad melange of carparks and sporting fields, concrete and bitumen here and there interspersed by pockets of what remained of the original bush, now broken, doomed remnants. Finding an old peppermint gum tree, whirling limbs and trunk sinuous marble and slate in the moonlight, she sat down beneath it.

The roots of the eucalypt were like great bird claws holding the tree to the earth while its writhing branches, reaching upwards, reminded Anna of a woman's fingers stretching into a new glove. There was something she once found vaguely erotic about old eucalypts, which she had then understood but no longer did, like a lost childhood language shared with vanished family. With their dreaming play of light and shadow and wind, their creak of branch and rattle and thrum of bark and shush of leaf, their spritely shadow-dance, old eucalypts always seemed to Anna individual and animated, expressing so many things and not one reducible to speech.

They simply were.

They were and they asked of others only this: are you?

Well, thought Anna, was she?

Yes.

No.

Maybe.

When she was little they went to church and church was a small wooden shed, and the only beautiful thing was the graceful eucalypts outside and their mottled shade, their smell, the thrum of their taut barrel, bird-call and bark-rattle, their elegant leaves so many lazing scimitars, the odours of dust and sap, the powdery funk of the ants and the spiders and the caterpillars that lived both within and beneath their maternal canopy. It was a universe overwhelming, intoxicating, euphoric.

She never smelt such things again.

She thought of all the insects then, so many that the EH Holden's windscreen would routinely be a mottled yellow and black mess of mangled cicadas or crickets or flying ants. Their small house in the hamlet by the beach would fill of a night with huge emperor gum moths as the family sat around playing crib. The ruggy thrum of their wings. She never saw such things again.

Their lives were small, thought Anna, how could they not be? Their smallness was what they were allowed, their smallness was what stunted growth was possible in the ruins and emptiness of the great blank that was their island's past. And trapped within, and them with it, a great forgetting that was somehow also a great memory if they could just dare open themselves up to it.

But the beach, the bush, the sea, the rivers, the insects and animals and fish, they were endless and vast. Their world was immense. It did not end. Their lives were small, their world was immense, and that world was endless in its wonder. When judged against history or politics or art, she and the people of her island were nothing. They had always been cast in the dock of the accused, guilty before trial. Convicts. Half-castes. Hicks. Inbreds. Two heads. They were defined as ugly and yet they lived in beauty. And in their world how large they became, how infinite they were, and in infinity, freedom, love, and hope were their birthright. The church was an empty shed and the beach was an overflowing universe, and there was their true religion, in the dunes and the marram grass and the boobialla groves, in the waves and the rips and the tide, the blinding sun and the gritty washes of sea wind, the late afternoon dazzle of the glazed sand ripples as the ocean receded, the taste of salt, the exultation of bodies diving into the first wave, falling and being lifted, the restorative power of the world.

Even in the worst of Anna's recent days the memory never left her. In the touch and salt scent of dawn wind, the light, the dazzle of midday, the rustle of tea tree, the shudder of eucalypt in the sea breeze, the sensual caress of a hot afternoon's shadow, she had felt whole. The world had only ever added and not, as now, subtracted.

On certain nights, when the moon was full, the families would gather at the beach and the men would walk a long seine net out into the silver and the white, past the breaking waves, dragging it through the sea perpendicular to the beach before hooping it into a great semi-circle and bringing it into shore where the women and children waited with buckets to fill. She would hold Ronnie's hand and they would watch never ceasing to be amazed at the miracle: life conjured out of empty water. For in the returning net were so many, many fish, so much food, and the goodness and joy and fecundity of it, the blessing of the sea, never left her.

9

She woke early that morning. When the phone rang it was as if she had known all night or perhaps forever that it would ring and Tommy would say those words—as if she were still dreaming and living in a world where she was propelled by events over which she had no power to halt or alter, only to repeat. From that moment everything seemed to accelerate, everything seemed weighted except her own movements, which weren't really movements at all but an uncontrollable drift past houses, streets, doors, corridors, lifts, faster, ever faster, towards that now familiar hospital room only to discover there that Francie had been transferred to the intensive care ward. As if in a dream that she seemed to both recall and be trapped within she found a heightened atmosphere in the ICU, and for all the hush, the solicitous staff, there was a large emotion, an unexpected feeling, and every act, every gesture, every whispered aside by nurses seemed freighted with fatal significance as, she supposed, it was.

Francie was asleep, or at least her eyes were closed. She now existed, or seemed to exist only as the anchoring point for a range of machines and stands with bags subtracting or adding various vital fluids, as if it were some elaborate embalming process and Francie already dead.

The thought came to her that the machines seemed real and of this world but their mother no longer did. One side of her face was blackened so badly it looked as if it had been in a car smash, an inevitable consequence of the blood thinners she had to take to prevent further strokes. The slightest knock and she bled. Her head seemed to have aged several decades overnight, all angles arched back on a pillow, her hair abruptly so thin it seemed to cobweb rather than cover her scalp, and her battered, hollowed face reminded Anna of nineteenth century photos of Native American chieftains: still, isolated, proud.

Doomed.

Francie's mouth and cheeks contorted with the act of breathing as if struggling to drag a load too great. Anna realised that dying—as she supposed Francie was hoping to, futilely attempting to escape life—was many, many things. But, mostly, it was hard work.

She took her mother's cold, clammy hand, ensnared in lines running back and forth to the machines that stood sentinel above. Her arm was covered in dressings for sores where her brittle skin had torn when nurses had moved or washed her.

Francie was no longer in one of her nighties but a hospital issue apron that afforded little privacy for her body. Through the side one breast was apparent. Anna, who had been small-chested, had always envied her mother's fuller figure. And having now lost one breast, Anna envied her mother that much more, for in spite of all her mother's losses her bosom remained. The skin of Francie's breast still looked soft and beautiful, somehow youthful, and that made Anna feel better, thinking of her mother as a young woman. And that day in that hospital in Hobart, it seemed strange to Anna that her mother's flesh, beyond her withered limbs and wizened face, looked so alive.

For her body was now doing what it had to do, evacuating life from flesh. When Anna rubbed Francie's legs they felt unnaturally chilled. Francie's colouring had changed from very pale to almost grey. Where once her body fought back, now it was simply abandoning position, extremity after extremity, limb after limb, like a retreating, disintegrating army refused surrender.

Francie's incoherent murmuring grew weaker and lower, Anna had to lean in so close to hear, and the only thing she was more conscious of than her mother's now occasional breath on her face was its terrifying absence, intervals that seemed to span minutes at a time.

They had saved her from death, but only, thought Anna, by infinitely prolonging her dying.

10

In the ensuing days their mother became so reduced in her capacities that she was fitted with an oxygen mask that attached to one more noisy machine. Francie, a nurse explained, was becoming too weak to breathe. They were trialling her on high flow oxygen therapy and hopefully they would soon have her back on the more conventional nasal prongs. But her face seemed to be shrivelling beneath the mask as though it were sucking life away rather than forcing oxygen in.

Doctors gave Anna disapproving and disappointed looks. There were several heated arguments in which the doctors said continuing dialysis was futile and cruel. Because in her heart she feared they were right, Anna had to kill that fear. She would hear herself yelling at the doctors that they wanted to murder her mother, that she would go to the papers, that it would be *all over the net*, that she would not hesitate to expose their cruelty.

As Francie withered away a little more each day she grew ever more attached to Davy, whose hand she refused to let go, and ever more unaware of Anna and Tommy. And the more she held on to the bearded boy and failed to acknowledge all that Anna was doing for her, the more determined Anna was that Francie should live. As the nurse had said that day now long ago, Isn't all living one long fight?

Yes, Anna had answered, the young woman's throwaway line sounding in her ears as a revelation—*one long fight . . . to live . . . to fight . . . to live.* Yes, yes, she thought, that was it! And what had been a throwaway line to the nurse became to Anna a profundity that both explained her mother's now ceaseless suffering and justified why she must continue to suffer into the foreseeable future.

To live . . . to fight . . . why live? . . . if not to fight?

It was as if a light had been shone into Anna's own darkness, even if what that light exactly revealed was for Anna impossible to say. The thing was that she could see it all clearly now, all that had been muddy and confused for so long was suddenly so obvious; everything that had been so difficult now seemed somehow easy, and nothing entered the ferocious self-enclosed circle that ran around and around in her mind.

To fight . . . to live . . . to live . . . to fight.

And yet again she began making calls to rally Tommy to stay the course, to find allies amongst prominent friends, threatening and cajoling, calculating and recalculating additional costs and how they might best be apportioned, and what new help might be required to help her mother live in order that her own life continue without facing the moment which terrified her above all; not the moment of her mother's death, but the moment after and the moment after that, the many gathering moments to which she could only offer up in opposition her mother's life, to which she could now see no end.

ELEVEN

Tossed and tumbled as if it were no more than a plastic bag, a tiny plane ploughed a stubborn if erratic furrow through dark storm clouds. It had taken no small effort on Anna's part to find herself in that ancient four-seat single-prop Cessna that wet spring. When she had asked Lisa Shahn if it would be possible to help count orange-bellied parrots, Lisa Shahn, to her great surprise, had said that they had just had a dropout from their next season's roster of volunteers. If Anna met the criteria and could spare the time, then the answer was yes. Thereafter followed an arduous fight over the winter to secure three months' leave without pay from her firm, the time-consuming tedium of procuring the appropriate police checks, medical certificates, first aid qualifications, to say nothing of a two-day orientation course.

And all that effort felt suddenly very questionable as, jammed in the back of the plane next to boxes of food and supplies, Anna bounced around nauseated and terrified.

Like a fucking airborne Hillman Minx, crackled Henny Carnevale over the plane intercom earphones. Henny Carnevale was old enough to remember Hillman Minxes. She was Anna's bird-watching companion, a sixty-seven-year-old printmaker from Adelaide, and she sat in the front seat next to a disturbingly young pilot who resembled a high school truant and together she and Henny were being flown into the wilderness of south west Tasmania to commence their duties as orange-bellied parrot counters.

The Hillman Minx abruptly tumbled out of the claustrophobic darkness of the clouds into a clear view of an immense wild vista of which they were now part: a large inland harbour surrounded by trackless hills of heath and buttongrass ceding to tea tree woods and rainforest, a world waving green in all its colours, rising up to snow-covered mountains in which not a human being lived. As the little plane steadied, Anna saw its tiny shadow tracking across the forests far below, a drop of spilt ink rolling across the page.

Christ, said Henny Carnevale, it's the end of the fucking world.

In summer, light planes brought tourists in, and more adventurous yachties found their way to the harbour.

But the sea and winds were too violent in early spring, the weather too vile, and no one appeared for days and sometimes weeks on end, and when the plane turned around and flew away leaving them with their supplies on the crude airstrip, Anna realised that they were alone there at Port Davey.

Six days later Henny Carnevale was flown out with suspected gallstones, leaving Anna on her own with only a half-smoked bag of Henny's very strong dope and a promise of a replacement volunteer as soon as feasible.

The weather immediately turned bad, wild south-westerlies, and no flight bringing the promised replacement volunteer had been able to get in since.

2

Anna's twice daily job was to check the nests. She would carry a ladder to each nesting box that had been placed in various trees and strategically sited poles. At each nesting box she would climb the ladder and, looking through a peephole, check the nest. Her task was to record the number of returned orange-bellied parrots and, later, any eggs and chicks.

But there was nothing to record.

November may have been the saddest month, but now it was early December, two weeks past the latest date the birds had ever before returned. Each nest Anna inspected was, as each nest had been since she arrived, empty.

Not one orange-bellied parrot.

At the end of two hours of traipsing and inspecting empty boxes, Anna reached the last, which was also the highest placed, found the rock used to somewhat precariously level the ladder, and set up.

She stood back, lit a joint of Henny's finest, which she had rolled at breakfast, balled her stiff shoulders, relaxed, and took in the improbable, immeasurable wonder of the plain and the mountains.

Joint finished, she climbed the ladder until she teetered slightly uneasily on the highest step. She lifted the nesting box's hinged flap and looked through the small hole into the darkness within. Her eyes adjusted. She was surprised to see slowly come into focus the very same window through which her mother had once glimpsed visions of the witch and Constantine.

Her chest tightened. She heard a growing drone. She shuddered. The ladder wobbled. She threw out her hand to steady herself, but it passed through the window as if it were open. And it was then, without her other hand to grab a rung and hold herself to the ladder, that Anna lost her balance.

3

She fell forward, following her hand into the hole and through the window. There was no sudden terror. There was a soft tumbling through silence, a matter of simultaneous stillness and movement. For the longest time Anna kept falling. And at the moment she was about to smash into the earth her body arced into a powerful swoop and she found herself flying.

4

She woke on a high plain of alpine heath, intricately leafed and finely flowered, a great bedspread of strange beauty. A low sun forced a russet beam between an inky sky and a distant mountain range onto an otherwise muted world. Flickering bars of shadow and light rolled over the heathland revealing bands of brilliant rust and iron and shimmering green. Far below, an otherwise black expanse of water she recognised as Port Davey glistened in sudden moments as if startled by the vivid light.

5

And only then did she see in the mid distance, standing on a dray, horse reins in hand, a fine-looking young man, sleeves rolled up his strong arms. It was Gus!—Gus somehow magically restored, full-bodied, wholly-faced, two-eyed Gus. Sitting behind him on the dray she recognised Terzo and Ronnie and Horrie, talking and laughing. Looking up, they saw her and waved her over. But when she went to walk towards them she couldn't. She was paralysed. They were calling to her. Come! Come! they were shouting. But no matter how she tried she couldn't move. Her family's shouts grew louder and ever more insistent. Come with us, Annie! But her body would not move and there was nothing she could do.

Finally, Gus leant down, spoke in a low voice to the others, stood back upright, and turning the horses and dray around began heading away, the others following on foot.

Long after they had vanished over a distant rise she watched where they had gone, unable to follow, frozen.

6

She heard a crack behind her. There was the most unexpected silence—and then another crack that felt closer, and when a third ricocheted off a rock not far away, Anna realised that somebody was shooting at her. The air was hissing with shots as Anna strained with every part of her being to move.

With an effort so painful that it felt it might tear her apart, one foot broke free and with it, a moment later, the other. She stumbled and almost fell, then finding her balance she staggered forward. She began to walk quickly then stride until she was running after Gus and her family, the shots now a fusillade raining around her.

She ran faster, ducking and weaving to evade the

bullets and using her arms and hand for balance until finally her gait altered into a stooped lope, her hand transformed into a paw and her arms into forelegs. As her shredded clothes fell away on the branches that tore at them, a striped hide began growing from her until she was a Tasmanian tigress with a newly born pup in her belly pouch, loping faster and faster.

Still the shots kept coming, it was inexplicable, a bullet ripped her belly pouch, killing her pup, and she was now the last, the only, the sole creature of her kind remaining in the universe yet the guns kept firing at her, she was running so hard that in each lengthening leap she began feeling less earth and more air until she was rising into the sky, flying until she was soaring, a wedge-tailed eagle, but she was again being shot at, she tumbled to earth she hid in remote mountain creeks as a giant freshwater crayfish where they came not stealthily with rifles but now noisily in machines that could fell and debough and debark a tree in a single long chew as if it were a corn cob a toothpick that could sweep aside a forest as if it were so many crumbs so much dust, until the rainforested banks, soft as down gentle as a caress, were no more than a violence of broken earth and burnt sticks, mudslides and floodings and she was choking on the silt until she escaped as a Tasmanian devil tearing at carrion on a back road. A handsome man saw her in his headlights, smiled, and accelerated. She was a spotted quoll sugar glider skink a spider beetle. And in each metamorphosis she was the last or the near last of her species.

She feared herself some carrier of doom.

But her ongoing flight was a life force beyond her powers to deny. She was myrtle. She was pencil pine. She was richea and scoparia and cushion plant, and each in turn vanished, tree grass moss; all these things in turn she became always had been without knowing, all of it all the world in her, all of it all of her vanishing—shot bulldozed logged mined developed poisoned choked beaten burning burnt.

There was no language of grief or loss that might encompass it. There was nothing there was everything there was nothing.

7

She was trying to outrun herself and failing. Words were collapsing, their job of conveying meaning meaningless in the face of all that was happening.

And she understood that they had not been expelled from Eden. That they had expelled Eden from themselves and there would be no return. Too late she realised it had always been here, within her grasp. Still she kept moving, staggering, her rate of movement measured in seasons centuries aeons, as an alpine grass, as a thousand-year-old lichen, as a microbe, as a spirit that might return as a warning a million years hence.

Her leg twisted and she fell. She threw an arm out but some strength, some resilience, some necessary speed of reaction was gone.

She realised that she was trapped in a thread of cellulite and carbon, fashioned over millennia into a serial organism that could survive firings, ice ages, the depredations of time and accidents of biology. But there was this time for the first time no possibility of regeneration.

8

Everything was vanishing around her as if in some fantastical story: fish, birds, plants, all were going or on the verge of extinction. And no one noticed, or only for a moment, and life went on until life was no more. She had grown up, she realised too late, in the autumn of things, an extraordinary world—its ancient rainforests, its wild rivers, its beaches and oceans, its birds and animals and fish, all were to her a path to freedom and transcendence, and none—she only now saw—were but a transitory wonder so soon to vanish until all that remained for a short time longer were human beings. But just for a short time. They could not survive alone, outside of the wonder—what could?—and so that time too would end.

Soon only wet gravel would remain, in which there would be visible for a short term specks of ash, transitory as despair. And then after a further time that too would vanish beneath more layers of dirt, rock, dust, a particularly thin band girdling the earth recording an unprecedented catastrophe rendered in meaningless detritus, so much ash and plastic.

And then there would be nothing.

9

In the general ward, Francie breathed in and out, machines exchanging fluid for fluid, gas for gas, substituting this for that, and in this way, long after Anna was dead, her mother continued to live.

She'll outlast the planet, said a cleaner looking up from her mop bucket.

Next to the bed sat her sole surviving son, a stocky middle-aged man who had introduced himself to her on a previous visit, with his nine-month-old granddaughter whom he worked diligently, patiently, to entertain with a shopping bag of dolls, picture books and toys. He had stuttered when they first met but there had been a change in him, and of late, though he said little, his stutter had receded. Every now and then the cleaner overheard him, as now, talking quietly to the old woman, a long soft sound.

Go with them, Mum, he was saying, you can go now everything is forgotten time is forgotten us and time forgotten this bed and window and the witch and Constantine forgotten even this feeling forgotten if you go go with the old people Francie go hear Ronnie laugh see your father ploughing red soil opening like a gift your father kneeling stories of us stories of miracles stories of birds stories of sun and colour and light you can go with them Mum they're waiting we'll meet you there. You can go, she could hear him whispering. It's all right.

As the cleaner squeezed the bucket rollers together with her foot and straightened up with the mop, he continued quietly incanting, calming, soothing. She watched him with the old lady and she watched him with the little girl, the tenderness with the mother, the care he took with the girl, the quality of his attention, and all this moved her. His kindness moved her. He had told her that after they were going to visit the little girl's father—his son. He was also in hospital in the mental health wing. The man said it as a statement of fact, without shame. His story—which he had briefly told her on another day—had been a simple one. The child's mother had rejected the child; she was badly ill, a personality disorder, mostly she was okay but lately, what with the smoke and the vanishings, she had fallen sick again; perhaps she would feel differently later, he didn't know. So, for now anyway, he had responsibility until one or both were better and ready to have her back. And if not, then he would raise her until whenever they were ready.

The cleaner said she was a lucky little girl.

He wasn't so sure. He hoped so. All he knew was that the things he didn't want to feel he didn't think about when he had her. Maybe, he said, as the little girl curled up in his arms and went quiet, he was the lucky one.

And realising she still had eight wards left to clean and her shift soon to end the cleaner went back to her work.

10

Some time later a doctor and two nurses came in. The doctor spoke quietly to the son who said nothing in reply, only nodded, stood up with the little girl in his arms, and moved away from the bed.

The son watched as the nurses stopped the fluids one by one. He watched as slowly, in silence, they went about taking out the drips and catheters from the old woman's flesh. He watched as the feeding tube was extricated from her mouth, and, last of all, the oxygen mask was taken off. He realised that the spider's web that had for so long enshrouded the old woman was gone. All that remained was a single drip administering Fentanyl.

Everyone stood still and, staring at her, listened.

She was breathing.

The doctor went to the drug charts at the end of the bed. He picked up the clipboard, checked his watch, the red band of which, the son noticed, was done up too tightly and cut into his fleshy wrist. The doctor put a big cross through page after page listing medications, signing at the bottom of each and adding the time.

And when he hung the clipboard back the son could not stop wondering why the doctor would not loosen his red watch band.

He watched as one by one the machines were switched off. The hum and whirr and infernal beeping ended. Its place was filled by silence.

Thank you, the son said. Thank you.

He watched as one nurse turned down the lights while the other pulled up the old woman's knee-high white pressure socks over the calves too withered to hold them in place. He watched as the next one straightened the sheets while the other propped the old woman up with pillows to make her comfortable. He watched as together they neatened her nightie and primped her red wool cardigan. He watched as they gently sponged her face and with the lightest of strokes brushed her hair into a cloud, as if to do otherwise might crumble it into dust.

When it was done the nurses and doctor stood back. Thank you, the son said. She looks good. Thank you.

After they left, he sat back down and took his mother's black-bruised hand. The room was very quiet.

Francie's breathing grew shallow and occasionally stopped for long periods altogether. She seemed calm. He tried to breathe with her. One nurse returned and asked him if he wanted anything—tea, coffee, biscuits?

He said he was fine.

And the little girl?

But she was sleeping, dreaming.

He sat there until darkness fell, trying to breathe with her, the child asleep in his lap, until he realised he was breathing alone. He sat for some time wondering why the doctor would not loosen his red watch band. Finally, he stood up. Cradling the slumbering child's head on his shoulder, he leant down and kissed the old woman on her cheek.

Tommy let his face stay there, touching Francie's for a good minute or more, the child's face next to them. He breathed in the mingled wild animal smell of his sleeping granddaughter and the close, cold odour of his dead mother.

The only sound was of rain on the window glass.

Steadying himself, he stood back up. For some time he stared at nothing and when the child woke and grew restless he left.

11

Lisa Shahn pulled her gaze away from the darkness, climbed back down the steps from the nesting box, and folded and dropped the ladder.

She wondered if the bird had been there when the poor volunteer, admittedly a strange woman, had her heart attack and dropped, it was assumed, like a stone to the earth, dead, according to the doctors, almost instantly. They said she would have not known a thing.

The sky was a black blue, there was so much brilliant black everywhere, the world seemed, for no apparent reason, suddenly extraordinarily alive. A light rain fell in the spring sun. She felt the strength of her limbs as her wet pants clung, and it felt good. A gust from the south west brought the brine of the Southern Ocean to her nostrils, a damp funk of salt and peat, and she breathed it in deeply. She was at that moment aware of everything.

12

The tiny bird, green as hope, newly arrived, two tiny black eyes brilliant as balls of dropped ink, held her head up a little longer until she was sure that the single astonished eye of the young woman staring into the darkness of her nest was gone.

Ruffling slightly, downy feathers appeared as she flexed on her haunches. She fluffed up in a controlled shudder, and then, dropping back down, settled her orange belly into a nesting position.

13

Without reason or thought, Lisa Shahn slowly got to her knees, sinking slightly in the mud, and, bowing her head, she waited for that moment when the universe might vibrate in and out and through her, that universe which she understood as her also.

That immense gift, the intense gratitude. The power of the woman in the world, the power of the world in the woman. She was kneeling, waiting. She was ready. She was, she realised with amazement, not downcast nor defeated.

ACKNOWLEDGEMENTS

[faded, illegible text]

ACKNOWLEDGEMENTS

I would like to thank Majda, Jean and Eliza Flanagan, Mary Voss, Dr Shannon Troy, Kev Perkins, Deb Taylor, Clara Farmer, Catherine Hill and Nikki Christer.

Scientists consider the orange-bellied parrot at risk of extinction within five years. In 2017 three adult female orange-bellied parrots remained in the wild. In 2019, because of a concerted national recovery program, twenty-three birds returned to Port Davey.